BETRAYED

BECA LEWIS

Published by:
Perception Publishing
https://perceptionpublishing.com

This book is a work of fiction. All characters in this book are fictional. However, as a writer, I have, of course, made some of the book's characters composites of people I have met or known.

ISBN-13: 978-0-9719529-8-0

Table of Contents

Prologue

Oblivious to the crashing of the waves that crested onto the shore only a few feet from the edge of his black robe, Ibris Elton, known as the Preacher, knelt in the wet sand on the island of Hetale. He shivered. Etar's blue light held no warmth, but bathed the sea, sand, and the white cliffs that rose behind him in an eerie blue glow.

Even when Trin, Thamon's second sun rose, there would be no warmth. The cold season had arrived, and both suns would never rise far above the horizon for many months. Ibris wrapped his robe around himself and raised the hood against the cold wind that flung the spray from the waves onto his back. It didn't help.

Ibris shivered not only because of the cold but because he knew that no matter what he chose, his people would suffer. Horribly. He moaned. He couldn't call them his people. They weren't his people. They belonged to Aaron now, and it was his fault.

The knowledge that he would suffer didn't matter to Ibris. For him, life was suffering. But that didn't mean he wanted others to suffer as he did. He had dedicated his life to alleviating the suffering of others.

But the way he had chosen had been the wrong way. He knew that now, but what could he do?

Aaron had granted him the warm season to convert the

Islands peacefully. And now the cold season was here, and the full conversion that Aaron thought had taken place on the Islands was an illusion.

Ibris wasn't sure how long it would be before Aaron discovered the truth, and his wrath would rain down on the Islands as it had on the rest of Thamon.

If he was the only one paying the price of his failure, he could bear it. But it wouldn't be him alone who suffered. No matter what he did now, he could never make up for the decision he had made so many years before.

It didn't matter that he had believed that he was doing the right thing. It didn't matter that he had only been a child. It didn't matter that his best friend and cousin, Dax, had chosen with him.

It didn't matter that he was an orphan, and the only adults he knew were the ones who told him he was doing the right thing.

It didn't matter because there had been times since then when he could have turned back, but he hadn't. He had continued down the same path because it was the only one he thought would work.

And if he was telling the truth to himself, he had been a coward. Afraid to change his mind.

But things had gotten worse. Stryker had found the top third of the pendant that was supposed to be hidden forever because of its deadly power. What if he found the other two pieces?

And then there was his cousin, Dax. They had once had the same mission. But Dax had changed. Dax had never learned the skill of mental manipulation, and as a result, had chosen the path of physical violence. Now they were both on the Islands together. He was trying to save the people, and Dax was trying to please the man that bound them.

But, Ibris could no longer hide from the fact that his choice to serve Aaron had failed. It was time to do what he should have done years before. He could only pray that he was doing the right thing now and that it wasn't too late.

Ibris buried his face in his hands and prayed. Prayed not to the God that he preached about, but to the God of his people. Prayed that his God, Ophy, the one he had known as a child, did not abandon him now. Prayed that Ophy, the goddess of light, would understand that he had not betrayed Her, but had tried to serve Her in his own way. Prayed for his family and friends who had been destroyed by Aaron and Stryker that they would forgive him. Prayed that he would find the strength to do what he had to do. Prayed that his new choice was the right one.

Above the roar of the waves, Ibris heard the bell of the Temple. It was time to return for the first service of the day. Once again, he would stand in front of the seven Kai-Via and preach the gospel of Aaron-Lem, trying to save the people from the wrath of Aaron and Stryker and know that he was failing the people. But not for long.

However, the people he was now choosing to betray were the most dangerous men on the planet Thamon. He would need help. Ibris prayed that he would find it.

One

Across the land bridge that tied the Islands of Hetale and Lopel together, Meg and Tarek stood on the edge of one of Lopel's cliffs watching the waves crash against the beach.

Meg's long dark hair and gray cloak flared behind her in the wind. She shivered, and Tarek pulled her close, wrapping his cloak around her.

Like Ibris, Meg shivered not only from the cold but because she knew what they had to do. They had to stop the destruction of magic. They had to stop Aaron and Stryker from taking over the Islands the same way they had taken over the rest of Thamon.

Sometimes Meg thought that what she and her friends were trying to do was hopeless. What gave her courage was what they had done so far and how much had changed.

Tarek was the biggest surprise. Meg leaned into Tarek, the top of her head reaching only to his shoulder. When Tarek looked down at her, she raised her green eyes to his blue ones and smiled.

Everything about Tarek felt like a miracle to Meg. Only a few months had passed since she had first seen him standing in the meadow. She hadn't trusted him. Well, she hadn't trusted anyone then.

Trying to escape what she had thought of as her parents' overbearing watchfulness, she had talked a portal maker in the dimension of Erda on the planet Gaia into sending her away to someplace beautiful and safe. Somewhere she could do whatever she wanted to do, whenever she wanted to. No more rules. No more laws.

Instead, he had tricked her. Meg knew it was her fault. She had tried to scare him into thinking she held a secret over him and would tell if he didn't help her.

What she had done proved to her now how stupid she had been. Threatening to tell the portal maker's secret meant he would make sure she could never return. The fact that she didn't know anything about him didn't help. Along with being stupid, she had been cruel and reckless.

Instead of getting what she wanted, the portal maker banished her. Yes, he sent her to a beautiful place, but it wasn't safe for her or any other Mage, shapeshifter, or wizard. She had arrived entirely unprepared for Thamon.

Unaware, and still stupid and reckless, she would have been captured and killed if it hadn't been for the unearned kindness of three other shapeshifters.

Ruth, Roar, and Wren found her and warned Meg of the danger to people like them. Then they taught her how to survive.

But they did more than that.

The three shapeshifters had taught Meg how to rebel in the right way and against the right people. They showed her what it meant to have friends, something Meg had never cared about before. Now, she had no idea what she would do without them.

******

Back at the cabin by the lake, those friends waited for Meg and Tarek to return.

All of them were restless. The decision to not do anything for the past month had been trying, even though they all knew it was a wise one.

They had all agreed to let Dax think he had succeeded in killing all of them in the earthquake and the flood that followed it. They needed him to relax his guard. And they needed to wait for Roar and the Mages they rescued to heal.

But for Wren, the waiting was becoming intolerable. She sat in the corner of the cabin, her cloak wrapped around her, staring at the fire, trying to calm herself down.

After they rescued the Mages from the prison camp, Wren had been as exhausted as everyone else and welcomed the time to rest.

But that exhaustion had passed weeks before. Now Wren wanted to be doing something, anything other than hanging out in the cabin, or the cave with the Mages.

While they waited, the cold season had arrived. That meant that the Preacher's agreement with Stryker for a peaceful conversion had come to an end. If Stryker discovered that the Mages and shapeshifters were still alive, he would do everything in his power to destroy them.

And now that Stryker had found the top third of the pendant, he was closer to having more power than any of them could overcome.

Wren started to pace the cabin, ignoring the looks from the others to sit down and be still. She knew they were as restless as she was, and understood how she felt. If Leon and his men were in the cabin, Leon would probably have succeeded in getting her to stop. But they weren't there. They were in the cave with the Mages, making sure they were warm enough.

Wren sighed to herself. She hoped that Meg and Tarek would return soon, and Tarek would tell them that the time had come to continue the rebellion. Otherwise, she thought she might explode. At the very least, shapeshift into a wild bird and fly like a crazy person through the air, even though they had all been forbidden to shift or use magic during this time, afraid Ibris, Dax, or Stryker would notice.

Before Tarek, Wren had been in charge. Although she appeared to be the youngest of the shapeshifters, she had a wisdom that made her new friends wonder if she was hiding her actual age. Only Ruth and Roar knew the whole story, and they wouldn't tell.

Turning over her authority to Tarek had been easy. From the moment she had seen him walking through the meadow outside the town of Woald, Wren believed that he was the one they had been waiting for, and so far he had proved her to be right.

But if he didn't do something soon, she might have to start something on her own.

Two

Outside the cabin, Suzanne and her new friend Silke Featherpuff sat on a tree stump watching Trin peek over the western horizon. Trin, along with the first sun Etar, wouldn't rise much further during the day. That meant that the Islands would not only be cold but would remain in perpetual twilight for the next few months.

Suzanne didn't like it. At all.

If she hadn't come to Thamon to rescue her wild-child sister, Meg, she could be back in Erda bathed in the warm sun, flying the skies with her dragon friends.

Instead, she was on this cold and dangerous planet waiting for the newly reformed Meg to return with that wizard, Tarek.

Suzanne knew that being irritable wasn't honestly how she felt. Well, maybe she did. Meg's new friendliness and the cold were not what Suzanne had expected. She thought Meg would be cold and the Islands warm. Both of which she was used to, and could handle. This reversal was unsettling.

The portal maker had warned her. Not about the weather, which she would have liked to have known. But he did tell her about the banning of magic. She decided to come anyway.

She didn't blame the portal maker for what he had done.

There had been many times in her life with her sister when she had secretly wished she could banish Meg. Send her away so she would not have to deal with her and all the trouble she caused.

But when that secret wish came true, Suzanne had discovered that she didn't want that after all. So, she had said goodbye to her parents and all her friends to come to Thamon. Her parents had been grateful. Her friends tried to talk her out of it.

"Is Meg worth it?" they had asked. When her friends realized that she wasn't going to change her mind, they wished her well, tears running down their faces.

It had been especially hard on the people she knew from both the Earth and Erda dimensions. Her friend from both, Kara Beth, had cried so hard that Suzanne had broken down and cried with her. But it didn't change her mind. The people of Erda were in good hands, and they didn't need her as much as her sister did.

Suzanne had arrived just in time to rescue Roar and Meg from the flood. It still amazed her that her sister had been willing to sacrifice her life to try and save Roar. Who had her sister become? Was that potential always there, or did she have to come to Thamon to find it?

If Thamon was Meg's destiny, did it mean that she too had a mission in Thamon? Not just to save her sister, and to help rescue the people of Thamon from the rule of Aaron and his religion Aaron-Lem, but maybe there was something for her here, too.

Suzanne softly snorted to herself. That would be different.

Beside Suzanne, Silke stirred, and Suzanne looked over at her in wonder. Silke Featherpuff was the perfect name for her. Silke had explained that all the Okan looked like her, except the male Okans didn't have her beautiful long hair that looked like feathers. Male Okans usually wore a cap. "Maybe to keep their head warm," Silke had said. But other than that, they looked much the same. They had human-like faces, but their bodies looked like tiny birds that blinked on and off.

Having lived in the Earth dimension, Suzanne knew what fireflies looked like, and when she explained to Silke that they also blinked on and off, Silke huffed and said it was nothing like that.

Okan blinking was not because they were looking for mates. That was not interesting to them at all. They blinked as a way to release the tremendous energy that ran through their bodies. "We are channels of light," Silke had said with a huff.

Whatever they were, Suzanne thought Silke was astonishing, and it amazed her that she and Silke had become friends.

In some ways she and Silke were complete opposites. When she shifted into a dragon, Silke could fit under the tip of one of her massive wings. In her human form, she could house Silke in her pocket.

Silke could shapeshift, too, but it was not something she liked to do and rarely did. But when she did, it was to something small, like a spider.

However, they had discovered that it was the fact that they were both tied in one form or another to someone else, that brought them together. Suzanne was tied to her sister, Meg. Silke was bound to Tarek.

Silke's tie had begun with Tarek's grandfather, and then his father, Udore, both wizards. Okans stayed through generations of wizards, but since Tarek had shown no desire to mate—let alone have children—Silke had decided he would be the last of her charges. However, now that Meg had arrived and Tarek, for the first time in his life, found himself interested in a woman, things were changing.

Suzanne and Silke sat impatiently waiting for the two people that ruled their lives because of their ties and loyalty to return and let them all know what they were doing next.

Suzanne longed to shift into a dragon, and perhaps find other dragons like her, but she couldn't. They had all agreed not to shift or do magic until they had a plan in place and were ready for the next phase of their resistance against Aaron-Lem's takeover of the Islands.

Silke, on the other hand, had to fly. She couldn't walk. Her legs were pretty but not useful for much other than balance when flying and standing on something. For now, to keep her magical footprint as small as possible, she rode on other people, usually Suzanne, when Tarek wasn't around.

Suzanne longed for a day when she could take off as a dragon, with Silke riding with her, skimming through the clouds, free as all beings are meant to be, not afraid of being shot out of the sky.

But first, they had to rid Thamon of Aaron and Stryker's rule, and restore the practice of magic to Thamon.

Across the lake, the sky darkened. Another storm, Suzanne thought, with a combination of fear and disdain.

The summer storms had been terrifying, but winter storms were far worse. The cabin and the cave were the safest places for them to be. They chose the cabin. At the end of the warm season, Leon and his men had strengthened the structure. Now the cabin stayed warm and dry during the worst of the storms. They had also added an entry room so that the winds didn't blow into the main room when the front door was opened.

As Suzanne and Silke came in through the first door, a flurry of sleet followed them in, along with a shout, "Hold the door!" Suzanne looked behind her to see Meg and Tarek running full speed, followed by a swirl of dark air filled with frozen crystals.

There is something very odd about these storms, Suzanne thought, as she hustled the two of them inside.

Was someone else on the island they didn't know about working dark magic? Or was it someone they already knew with powers more significant than they thought? Or perhaps the Islands trying to get rid of them? Either way, it was time to do something before it got worse.

Tarek turned to Suzanne and nodded. It was his way of telling her that he knew what had to happen, and he was ready.

Three

He couldn't stop thinking about it. Rationally, Stryker knew that it was a bad idea to be in love with something so much that he had to keep checking to make sure it was still there. But his passion for it was not rational. Even he knew that. But Stryker didn't care. He loved it. It loved him, too. He was sure of it.

Sometimes he would find himself standing in front of a mirror, shirt off, staring at the pendant hanging around his neck. Other times he would lose track of what people were saying to him as he thought about the necklace hidden beneath his robe.

There was nothing spectacular about the way it looked, especially since most of it was missing. A tiny voice inside of Stryker sometimes whispered that he should return it to the cave where he had found it. It would tell him that there had to be a reason why someone had hidden it in the first place.

But Stryker barely listened to that voice. He believed that it was testing him. Instead, he would remind himself that there was a reason why he had found the magical map on his seventh birthday. It was his destiny.

He was supposed to bring the pieces of the pendant together again. He had been chosen to achieve the ultimate ability to control people. It was his mission, divinely inspired, and he wasn't going to walk away from that.

The whisper from within would counter that argument by telling him that the pendant was controlling him. He knew that was a lie, too. It was probably implanted by the people who had hidden the pieces of the necklace in the first place.

Stryker believed that whoever they were had wanted to make sure that only the right person, an extraordinary person, would be able to overcome the obstacles placed in the path of putting the pendant back together again. He knew that he was that person. After all, look at all that he had already overcome.

First, he had found the map. On his seventh birthday, he had been smart enough to follow the signs that led him to the map hidden under a rock in the woods. It was the map that would eventually lead him to the top third of the necklace. But not right away.

After finding the map, he spent years researching what the map was showing him and what it meant. To make it even more complicated, the map itself was a mystery. It was never the same each time he looked at it.

Of course, he realized that made the map magical and magic was banned on Thamon. He found it delightfully ironic that he was the one in charge of making sure that there was no magic left on Thamon.

Stryker laughed to himself. Right. Magic was supposed to be banished, and it was. But he knew there were people in power who practiced magic. The banishing of magic was for everyone—except those with power.

What made the finding of the pendant so delicious was knowing that he was now one step closer to having more power than anyone else on Thamon.

Yes, the map was always a challenge, but one he could

handle. However, because it was never the same, it took him years before he discovered that the map was pointing him to these two remote Islands, Hetale and Lopel.

That gave him his next challenge. He had to convince his friend and conspirator, Aaron, the God of Aaron-Lem, to leave the Islands alone until they finished conquering the rest of Thamon. That done, he then had to convince Aaron that Ibris' idea to peacefully convert the Islands rather than using the violence they had employed everywhere else, was a good one.

It was a double deception. Ibris thought that Stryker had agreed because Stryker was doing him a favor, and Aaron thought it was because Stryker wanted to live on the Islands and didn't want its beauty destroyed. Because they were friends, and Stryker had helped Aaron make up the religion of Aaron-Lem and then lead the destruction of anyone opposed to it, Aaron thought that he was doing Stryker a favor.

Both Aaron and Ibris were wrong. Stryker chuckled to himself, pleased at how easily he had manipulated them both. Two of the most powerful people on Thamon.

Aaron was the leader of Aaron-Lem. Aaron, a self-professed god who could do anything, and Ibris, as the most influential Preacher of Aaron-Lem, were supposed to be the masters of manipulation.

It pleased Stryker immensely that even before he had found the pendant, he had tricked them both. Now that he had found the top third of the necklace, he was one step closer to becoming the one ruler of Thamon, able to manipulate anyone, at any time.

The moment he had placed the slim gold chain around his neck, the pendant had nestled into his chest as if it had lived there forever.

That only increased his belief that he was the chosen one.

He would overcome whatever other obstacles were placed in his path to prove it. There was no way he would fail.

However, the desire to find the next part of the pendant kept him awake at night. The map would not reveal the next hiding place, and he was going out of his mind with anticipation and boredom. Yes, boredom. There was nothing to conquer. All the Mages had died in the explosion set off by Dax.

Waiting for the map to reveal to him where to find the next part of the pendant was making him crazy. He needed some form of distraction. Maybe he should spend a little time finding out if either Ibris or Dax were planning something. If they were, he would have a good reason to torture them, and that would relieve some of his boredom. The idea was so appealing, Stryker almost hoped that they were. Even if they weren't, maybe he could pretend that they were, and torture them anyway.

Stryker reached beneath his robes, fingering the pendant, waiting for an answer, but it remained silent. Even the voice was quiet.

Four

Dax stood at the back of the Temple watching Ibris as he stared out the window at the storm. Ibris didn't move, acting as if he hadn't felt Dax's presence. They both stood there lost in their thoughts until Ibris finally turned, and the two of them stared at each other, perhaps sizing each other up and wondering what the other was thinking.

Neither one of them had on the black hooded robes that hid their identity from the people. There was no one in the Temple to see, and they certainly didn't have to hide who they were from one another. They had known each other since they were babies. Their fathers were brothers, and when they were young their families had lived together, farming the same land that had been in their family for generations.

However, Dax's father grew tired of farming and moved the family to the city. After that, the families only saw each other every few years, something that both boys regretted. They had been the best of friends then.

If someone had been in the Temple, they would not have thought they were related. Ibris looked like his father, tall and slim with blond hair and blue eyes.

Dax took after his mother's side of his family, powerfully

built and close to the ground with dark brown eyes that showed flakes of gold when he was angry.

That wasn't the only thing that set them apart. Even as children, Ibris had preferred the realm of internal thoughts like his mother. Dax was full of fire and the desire to do something. Dax was a daredevil. He was constantly doing things that scared his parents, like jumping out of trees and leaping across chasms. Dax was always searching for the rush of adrenaline. Ibris was happy with a book, sitting under a tree.

What frustrated Dax the most was his inability to tempt Ibris to join him. No matter how much he taunted Ibris to try dangerous things with him, he could never convince Ibris to do it. Ibris would smile and put his arm around Dax and tell him that Dax was the brave one and how much he admired him.

Ibris claimed that he was too much a coward to do those physically dangerous things that brought Dax so much joy. That response only made Dax more furious and jealous. Even then, Dax felt as if Ibris was the one with all the courage. He was the one who chose his own path no matter what others said or did.

Over the years, that rift grew in Dax's mind. He believed that Ibris thought that he was better than Dax. But he could never tempt Ibris into admitting it or acting like it. Dax hated that Ibris kept on caring about him no matter what he did. Each time Ibris forgave Dax for being upset with him, it only increased Dax's frustration.

Ibris became the symbol of everything that Dax could never be, so he let the bonds of their friendship loosen and fall away. After all, they were growing up to be different people. Dax loved the city the same way his father did, and Ibris loved the country.

In time, Ibris and Dax lost touch with each other. Then the unthinkable happened. Both of their towns were destroyed, and both of them lost their entire family and all their friends. As luck would have it, Dax and Ibris were the only ones who had survived the destruction. Stryker's men had rescued them and then had brought them to Stryker as orphans.

From that moment on, they belonged to Stryker. Back then, they were both so grateful to Stryker they would have done anything to please him. After all, he had rescued them and brought them together again as a family. As they grew up, Stryker took care of their every need. All the while, he was training them to be part of Aaron-Lem. At first, they learned the same things, but then Ibris began to excel in converting people to Aaron-Lem through his preaching. Dax had no talent for it, so he became part of the violent conversion process.

Now, as adults, Ibris was Stryker's most effective preacher, and Dax was the head of his best Kai-Via, the enforcers of Aaron-Lem. And now they were together again on the Islands because Stryker had sent them there. Stryker was still ordering their lives around. They were still doing what he asked of them.

Now, when Ibris preached, Dax stood behind him among the seven Kai-Via. To Dax, this was once again an insult to him. He was always behind Ibris.

However, even after all this time, even with all their differences, and the growing disparity in their abilities, Ibris still opened his heart to Dax whenever he saw him. And Dax knew that Ibris saw him. Not just the physical outside, but what had happened to Dax inside of himself.

Ibris knew that Dax was angry and bitter. In spite of that, Ibris still loved him. The part of Dax that still lived inside of him as the adventurous and joyous boy he once was, sometimes responded in kind. It would flicker briefly and then it would be gone again,

But Dax didn't think that Ibris knew how determined he had become to take power away first from Stryker and then

Aaron. Dax knew that the craving for power was eating away at him, that eventually, all that would be left would be the need for more control, just like Stryker and Aaron.

Dax knew that someday that boy Ibris knew would be gone forever. He knew that letting him go that way was a betrayal to who he had been. It was a betrayal to his dead family, who would be appalled at the choices that he was making. But Dax didn't care. He knew things that Ibris didn't know.

Dax knew how and why their families had died. To Dax, that was the bigger betrayal. A betrayal that he could never forgive. And he was going to destroy everyone that made that happen. If Ibris insisted on supporting Aaron and Stryker, he would destroy him too.

The question that haunted Dax was if he should tell Ibris the truth about their families. Would Ibris betray him if he did?

As Dax watched Ibris, he admitted to himself that he was afraid that someday Ibris would turn to look at him and see only the evil man he had become. Then, Ibris would no longer smile at him because he would know and accept that Dax had become the enemy.

Five

While the storm raged outside, inside the cabin the moss stuffed between the logs of the walls kept it cozy and warm. Although the sound of the hail pelting the roof sounded like a giant was throwing stones at the cabin, they all did their best to ignore it and keep their attention on the crackling fire.

Leon had returned to the cabin right after Meg and Tarek with his arms full of leaves and tubers promising that he would turn it all into something delicious for them to eat.

So while the rest of them sat around waiting for the storm to be over, Leon cooked what he brought in a big pot that hung over the fire. Leon being there made the cabin even more crowded, but no one complained.

Meg loved to watch Leon as he cooked. It helped take her mind off of the thoughts that kept running around in her head. Although a big man, Leon moved like a ballet dancer around the fire stirring the kettle and adding herbs to it as he tasted it.

Meg had seen Leon lift logs over his head, yet he handled his cooking with a gentle grace. It was this marriage of opposites into one whole person that made Leon both fascinating and inspiring to Meg.

She hoped that she could learn to do the same within herself if she watched him enough.

Meg knew that Leon had been the chef on the ship that had brought Stryker to the Islands. Leon and his men had served Stryker on the voyage, knowing that once they arrived, they would be part of the resistance against him and Aaron-Lem.

The men had played their role so well, Stryker had never suspected Leon and his team of eight men to be traitors to Aaron-Lem. Even when one of Leon's men, Vald, allowed himself to be caught and tortured, Stryker and Dax hadn't known that he had been one of the men on the ship.

Vald had survived Dax's torture thanks to Silke and her spider bite that had numbed his senses. Vald's shredded feet had healed enough for him to wear shoes again, although his feet were still tender, and depending on the weather, he still limped.

However, no one had ever heard him complain. Instead, Vald, like the rest of Leon's men, was more determined than ever to take back the Islands, and eventually, the planet of Thamon.

As Leon ladled out the stew he had made, Meg thought about how grateful she should be for being part of this community. And she was.

However, even though thankful for having friends, sharing food, and a group that took care of each other, it still felt foreign and often uncomfortable for her. It was a whole new way of life, and not one she had ever aspired to be part of.

Her thoughts returned, where they often did, to what she had been like before arriving on Thamon. Being with Tarek out on the cliff had only reminded her of what she used to be like and now apparently wasn't anymore. She still wasn't sure that was okay with her.

She had loved being a wild child. Yes, she had been impossible to contain and not interested in anyone but herself.

However, she had reveled in being that wild child. She had

been happy with who she was and what she did, and she hadn't cared if that made everyone around her unhappy. She had been so much trouble that her parents had taken her to another dimension to get her away from Erda.

They thought that in a new environment she would calm down, or at least they would be able to control her better. But the opposite had occurred. She had acted out even more in the new dimension. She had loved that it was a new landscape to explore and a new group of people to annoy.

Finally, her parents gave up. Meg wasn't better. They had even less power over her. Besides, they had missed the companionship and support of other shapeshifters and their other daughter, Suzanne. The one that Meg resented and called a goody-two-shoes.

Eventually, her parents gave up and returned to Erda.

That was the chance that Meg had been waiting for. She had forced them to return on purpose by acting out even more in the new dimension. Meg wanted to escape her parents and all the rules around being a "good" shapeshifter more than ever. She didn't want to be a good shapeshifter. She didn't want to be someone who followed the rules and helped people. She wanted to be free to do whatever she wanted to do whenever she wanted to do it.

Barely a week back in Erda, Meg had searched out the portal maker and tricked him into sending her to someplace where she could be free forever. But the portal maker had tricked her instead and sent her to Thamon, a planet where magic was banned, and Mages and shapeshifters were hunted and killed. A world where Aaron and Stryker controlled everyone through an extremely effective combination of mental manipulation and violence.

At first, it didn't seem so terrible, especially after she met

Ruth, Wren, and Roar. Meg had decided that with their help, she could learn how to adjust to her surroundings. That had happened, but not the way she thought it would.

It had all turned out to be the opposite of what Meg felt that she wanted. Her wild-child image started to fade, and she began making friends.

But before that, she started to lose her shapeshifter powers. The one thing that had defined her whole life started leaving her. At first, her abilities vanished only at night, and then they began to disappear during storms. It was worse now because of the cold months. It was sometimes too dark during the day for her to shapeshift.

Recently, she had discovered to her growing horror, that she was not always able to shift at all. Meg didn't want to admit it to anyone, but she was terrified. Her body was betraying her. Who would she be without her powers? She would be Ordinary.

It didn't matter that she was learning that being ordinary wasn't considered by others as a terrible thing. That Ordinaries like Leon and his men had other abilities that were just as wonderful. It was the feeling that what made her who she was, was slipping away that gave her nightmares.

And now sitting in the cabin where she should be warm and grateful, she felt as if she would jump out of her skin, or snap at one of these people who had befriended her. The warm cabin, the good friends, Tarek caring for her, and Leon's food should be making her happy, and yet, sometimes, it felt like a slow form of torture.

Tarek looked at her from across the room, and she knew that he was worried about her. Would she break under the strain of becoming someone new? She didn't know the answer, so she couldn't give him any more than a tiny smile, trying to force as much happiness into it as possible. She knew that she wasn't fooling him.

   She hated that she was giving him something else to worry about. After all, his mission was to rescue a whole planet from the grip of Aaron and Stryker, not save a person like her, who probably wasn't worth it.

Six

While Meg reviewed her life, the Mages waited in the cave, Ibris and Dax sized each other up in the Temple, Stryker pondered the map and Aaron sat on his throne, an ocean away. Plotting his next move.

Aaron smirked to himself. Perhaps other people wondered if what they were doing in life was making them happy, or if they were doing the right thing. He didn't. Everything about his life made him happy, and he always knew he was doing the right thing.

Who wouldn't be pleased with this, he thought to himself. Everything in Thamon revolved around him. His choices had always been perfect. He had devoted disciples, who named themselves the Blessed Ones—disciples who were willing to be rendered blind so they would have the honor of serving him.

Across Thamon, his Preachers and his Kai-Via made the people happy by converting them to Aaron-Lem. His religion.

He, Aaron, was the God that they worshiped. No other gods were allowed. Any mention of those old gods was an automatic prison and possible death sentence. Not that the people talked about those other gods anymore. He gave them what they needed. They didn't need anyone else. Their lives were perfect because of him, and they knew it.

Three times a day, a bell would ring and his people would stop where they were and bow to him to thank him for the blessings that they received. Sometimes their faith and gratitude were so intense he could feel it flowing across Thamon straight into his heart. It was a magnificent feeling.

All that good-will directed to him from the millions of converts to Aaron-Lem fueled his knowledge that he had done the right thing. He had cleansed the planet of everyone who wanted to worship other gods.

Although some people only wanted to be left alone to live the life that they wanted to live without worshiping anyone or anything, it didn't matter. They were also gone. He had eliminated from Thamon everyone who didn't succumb to Aaron-Lem. Now it was as if they never existed.

Yes, he was happy. Yes, he had made all the right choices in his life. He had risen from nowhere and become the God of Thamon. Unbeatable. He would not let the news that his spies brought him take away his happiness or his certainty.

For a moment, a dark cloud passed over Aaron's features as he thought about what he had learned a few days before.

Once again, he was grateful that the Blessed One washing his feet couldn't see anything. It was good for them, too, because if he had noticed that Aaron was even temporarily unhappy, Aaron would have had to kill him. He couldn't afford even the smallest hint of doubt that he wasn't eternal and all-powerful among his followers.

So while the Blessed One finished what he was doing and shuffled backward out of the room, replaced by another Blessed One bringing him afternoon tea, Aaron reviewed what his spies had told him. Aaron wasn't sure he believed them. He didn't want to. But he had to entertain the possibility that they were not mistaken. Aaron was sure they wouldn't have lied to him. They knew the consequences of doing that.

Could it be true? Had some people in Thamon escaped the conversion and were in hiding? His spies had recovered some writings that indicated that they had. The papers claimed some people had seen signs of what was coming, and hidden before his conversion forces arrived.

But there was no proof. It was all speculation. No one knew anything for sure. If the people had escaped, no one knew where they had gone, or how many of them there were.

Aaron knew that even if there were people still hiding from him, there couldn't be many of them. When they found them, it would be easy to eliminate them all, since they would only be Ordinaries.

Stryker had assured him that all the Mages were gone. They were captured, imprisoned, tortured, and then killed. That thought made Aaron snicker with happiness again.

However, he needed to decide what to do about the news. He first had to decide whether or not he should kill the spies that had brought him the news. He didn't want them telling anyone else about what they had found. On the other hand, they were already up to date, and he wouldn't have to find someone to take their place.

In the end, he had let them live. But first, he threatened to kill them and their families and friends if they shared the information with anyone other than him. He would let them live, for now. But if they didn't return with the information about where those people were hiding, he would kill their family members one by one.

The men had bowed and scraped their way backwards out the room. Because no one could ever look upon him—he was a God after all—they had been blindfolded.

He couldn't have them blinded. That would hamper their efforts. So a blindfold had to do.

The combination of not being able to see where they were going, and the relief that they were not dead, caused them to stumble and fall against each other. The sight was so ridiculous that Aaron started laughing, but when it didn't stop, he grew angry and called in a Blessed One to lead them out.

The blind leading the blind, Aaron thought. He was the only one with eyes to see.

Now that the spies had left again to search out the hidden Ordinaries, Aaron sent a message to his long-time conspirator, Sawdi Frey, to join him for dinner. There was a possibility that the Warrior Monks would have to be brought out of their semi-retirement. If that happened, Sawdi would be in charge of them, once again.

Aaron kicked at the Blessed One in front of him, causing him to fall backward and then stepped on his hand on his way out of his throne room. The Blessed One bowed in Aaron's direction, ignoring the pain in his hand. Aaron didn't notice. He was too busy thinking about what he and Sawdi would have for dinner when he got there. It would probably be a few days before Sawdi arrived. Perhaps in the meantime, he would have some fun and go hunting for what they would eat.

First, he had to find some poor fool to fetch Sawdi. Sawdi would know what to do with him once he delivered the message. It would be an excellent way to get rid of the stable boy who wasn't working out well.

Aaron was pleased with himself. He could accomplish more than one thing at a time: arrange for his horse and send out that fool boy to a fool's errand. The humor of it tickled his fancy. Maybe he would stop off to see the women of the Blessed Ones. He could get tickled in another way while he waited.

Seven

Sawdi Frey stood at the door of his cottage and watched the messenger struggle up the road. Sawdi had made the road as impassible as possible on purpose. He had been living by himself for almost a year and had finally adjusted to the quiet life.

He didn't want company. He hated it when someone did find him. It meant that he would have to get rid of them in a way that didn't call attention to himself. He didn't mind eliminating them. It was the extra effort of hiding what he had done that he didn't like.

The men who had helped him build his cabin no longer existed. He had kept them on the land until they finished the cabin, not letting them leave. After that, he had buried them together. If there was such a thing as an afterlife, Sawdi hoped they liked being together.

The back of the cabin was nestled up against a mountain, almost at the top. The back room of the cabin was built inside the mountain. A passageway from that room led to an opening nearly a half-mile away.

If someone stumbled on the cabin, it looked unimposing, just as Sawdi wanted it to look, but if necessary, he could escape in a hurry.

Watching the messenger struggle up the path was amusing. Sawdi knew that the messenger had to leave his horse at the bottom of the hill. The path was pitted with holes and deep crevices too dangerous for a horse. It could barely be called a path. Actually, it wasn't one. It was an obstacle course. It was not the path Sawdi used to get to and from his cabin the few times that he left it.

But even if the messenger had found the real path, he wouldn't have made it more than a few feet before he would have been hanging by his heels from the nearest tree having stepped into one of the traps set by Sawdi. As it was, no one looked for another way to the cabin. Most people just avoided the path altogether after seeing what it looked like. That was the point, after all. Keep people away.

Sawdi encouraged the rumors about who lived at the top of the path, hidden in the woods. He had heard he was an evil wizard, a cunning warrior, and a crazy man who killed everyone he saw. No one knew if any of those rumors were true, but no one wanted to find out for sure.

Since this messenger was still coming—having fallen a dozen times, and was now covered with mud and scratches—Sawdi knew that his retirement time must be over. Only Aaron would inspire enough fear to make sure the messenger did what he was supposed to do.

Of course, Aaron could have used another way to reach him. They had more than one way to get in touch with each other. But Aaron would have loved the idea of sending someone on this almost impossible mission.

Aaron had called on him a few months ago, worried about Stryker. Although Sawdi had thought there might be a reason for worrying, he didn't say so. Working with Aaron was like working with a viper, and if anyone was going to be a viper,

Sawdi wanted it to be him. So he had assured Aaron that he was mistaken about Stryker.

Besides, it annoyed him that Aaron still thought that he had to train him. From the beginning, Sawdi had set up that false premise so that Aaron would not realize that he was the real power of Aaron-Lem, not Aaron. So it was his own fault that Aaron thought he was in charge. It didn't mean that he liked it. However, since Aaron had managed to make himself the God of Thamon with his help, Sawdi had decided to let it be, for now. He had no desire to be known or worshiped, which is probably why Aaron trusted him, and no one else had heard of him.

Aaron believed that Sawdi didn't want to take over Thamon, but he knew that Sawdi did love a challenge that involved pain. Not for him. For others.

Although Sawdi never asked himself if what they had done was worth it, once in a while, he would think back to where it had begun with him, Aaron, and Stryker. The three boys had found each other after they had been sent away to school. All three of them for the same reason—to get them out of the way. They were too hard to handle, and no one wanted them. The school promised to reform them, and their families washed their hands of them.

Perhaps the school didn't mean to teach them how to be what they became. Maybe they were already predators, and being together only made it more visible. Perhaps the sadist practices at the school fueled a fire that already burned within them. Their families had turned their backs on the three boys. They couldn't control them, so they let the school do it.

On days that everyone else had a visitor, the three boys did not. They were left alone to come up with ways of entertaining themselves.

Although Aaron thought he was in charge of their

adventures, it was Sawdi who had suggested them. And those adventures were always based on the practice of controlling others.

It was not surprising that Aaron became the head of Aaron-Lem. He was the one who wanted to be visible. Under Sawdi's guidance, the three of them had designed the religion together. They put in everything they knew about controlling others—things learned in school and things they had learned through experimentation. Now Aaron-Lem was the only religion allowed on Thamon, which was the intent after all.

But once Thamon was entirely converted, what had there been left to do? Magic was gone, the people who wouldn't convert were dead. Or at least that was what Sawdi had thought until a few months ago when Aaron had called on him to talk about Stryker.

Sawdi told Aaron there was nothing to worry about, but he had questions that he asked himself. *Was Stryker up to something? Were all the Mages really dead?*

These were questions that had turned the fire back on inside of him. He had returned to his cabin and waited for what would come next.

Sawdi wondered what Aaron would do if it were true that Stryker had turned against him. What did he want Aaron to do about it? The prospect of moving the pieces of the world around to his liking excited him.

As the messenger tripped one last time and ended up crawling the last few feet through the mud to the door, Sawdi realized that he was happy to see him. It meant that his boredom had come to an end.

Eight

While the storm raged outside, inside the cave, the Mages and their families huddled around the central fire. After he found the cave, Tarek had used his magic to provide light and to keep it warm. But the dampness in the air remained, which meant fires were part of daily life. And like all their supplies, it was Leon and his men that brought them the wood that they needed.

The men had supplied the tents, sleeping bags, blankets, clothes, and food that had been waiting for them when they had arrived in their new home in the cave. At the time, they had all been so exhausted and beaten down, that they had barely noticed. All they knew was that they were no longer being starved or threatened by Dax and his prison guards.

The prison camp had been a living nightmare. One they couldn't wake up from. Dax had made sure that they were drugged continuously so that there was no chance that they could use any of their magic skills to escape. However, the drugging and abuse were not limited to the actual Mages and shapeshifters. It had extended to their children and spouses. Dax had been taking no chances of anyone escaping. If you were related to a Mage, you were dangerous.

There had been hundreds of Mages in their community before the arrival of Aaron-Lem. Now there were only a few dozen left, all living in the cave.

Most of the captured Mages had died in the prison camp. But even after their rescue, others had died in the cave. Some of the rescued had given up, no longer willing to live in the world that Aaron had created for them. Others were just too far gone, and nothing anyone did could save them. The mourning for their lost ones was a constant companion for all of them.

Once the drugs worked their way out of their systems, the remaining Mages were ready to make some decisions. What they needed to decide was something they wanted to talk about while Tarek and the rebels were busy doing something else. The raging storm gave them the perfect opportunity. Although some of Leon's men always stayed with them in the cave, they were too busy monitoring the storm and watching the water rise, to pay much attention to the gathering around the fire.

It wasn't that the survivors weren't grateful for the rescue. They were. But whatever they did next, they wanted it to be their own decision. Never again did they want to be at the mercy of anyone else's plans for them no matter what their intentions were. And no matter what each person decided, the group as a whole would support each person's decision.

Some of them wanted to stay and fight with the rebels. Aaron-Lem was a poison that had infected the entire planet. They wanted to be part of its elimination.

Others wanted to stay safe. They wanted to take their spouses, children, and partners, and hide somewhere that Aaron and his Kai-Via would never find them. They hoped there was such a place.

They had heard that there were people who had anticipated the coming of Aaron-Lem and were in hiding. They wanted to join them.

This meeting was about making those final decisions. Who would stay, and who would go. No matter what each person decided, it would be hard for everyone. Their hardship had bonded them together forever. It would be even worse for some of them because they knew that what they decided would break up families and split apart friends. It was a somber group that gathered around the fire.

This was not the first meeting that they had held. Over the last few weeks, they had several gatherings. Those meetings had been mostly focused on their needs living in the cave. But as they got better and they realized that they would be making life-changing decisions, the survivors knew that they needed a leader to help them accomplish whatever each person decided.

It took only one meeting to decide who that leader would be. It was a unanimous, if slightly surprising, decision. But once her name was introduced as a possibility, there was minimal discussion. With a quiet, hands-up vote, they had chosen Wren to be their guide in this new world.

To an outsider, it might have appeared to be an unlikely choice. Wren was not one of them. She was not a survivor of the prison camp.

But the selection of Wren was based on more than one factor. It started with the fact that Wren was a shapeshifter. One of possibly only four remaining shapeshifters in all of Thamon. Her ability to be anyone or anything gave her an advantage, and they needed every advantage they could get.

But it was more than that. They had all known Wren for long time. They knew that although she presented herself as a young woman, she wasn't. She had been a young woman when their grandparents were alive. How that could be possible, or where she had initially come from, no one knew. But they did know her heart and her courage.

Wren's latest rescue of them was not the first time she had rescued them. Not only from the Aaron-Lem and its watchdogs the Kai-Via, but from the times when practicing their magic had not gone well.

No one was surprised that Wren had escaped being captured. They knew how wise and resourceful she could be. Those that were thinking of staying to fight Aaron-Lem knew they could trust her to save them again if necessary. And the Mages who didn't want to stay knew that she would find a way to get them to safety.

Now, all they had to do was ask her.

Nine

The storm had gone, leaving behind a thin sheet of ice on everything. It wouldn't last long. As weak as the suns were at this time of year, they would still melt off the ice within a few hours. In the meantime, the ice and the low light turned the world into sparkling crystal shapes.

Meg pulled her cloak tighter around her and shivered in the cold air. It felt as if she would never get warm in this cold season. She longed for summer, but it was months away.

Only Silke seemed to be immune to the cold. Of all of them, being so small, it would seem that she would be the most likely to be affected, but instead, Silke seemed to thrive no matter what the weather. Now her blinking on and off just added to the magical effect of the ice-covered world around them.

As soon as the storm had stopped, everyone who had been in the warm cabin made a rush for the door, choosing the cold air over one more minute in the confined cabin space.

However, it didn't take long before Leon had a fire roaring for them outside by the lake. Meg thought he had become the master of fires and was once again grateful for Leon's abilities.

As they stood around the fire, warming hands and staring at flames, Meg was beginning to think that was all they were ever going to do, stare at fires.

She was of two minds about it. Her restless nature hated the idea of doing nothing. However, the memory of what had happened at the prison camp when she had attempted to rescue Roar and the awareness of what was coming as they continued the resistance made her think that perhaps it wouldn't be a bad thing to stare at fires for a little longer.

Ted, one of Leon's men, had returned from the cave and said that the survivors were requesting that Wren visit them as soon as possible. Looking over at Wren standing by the fire, Meg thought that Wren didn't look at all surprised. Feeling Meg's eyes on her, Wren lifted her gray eyes and smiled at her.

Meg thought back to the first time she had met Wren and the other shapeshifters. They had surprised her at the deserted building where she had been living. And after gaining her trust, they had explained to her the dangers of what was happening on Thamon. If it hadn't been for the three of them, Meg knew she would have ended up in the prison camp. Or worse. She had been reckless in using her shapeshifting abilities, and sooner or later, the Kai-Via would have found her.

Instead, the three shapeshifters had befriended her. The word "befriend" was an idea and concept that had never interested Meg before. Now she knew she wouldn't be alive without it.

As Meg looked at her, Wren shifted into a red fox, and then back to herself, or at least how she presented herself. Her shifting got everyone's attention, and Wren laughed. That was precisely what she had wanted.

"I think I know what the survivors want to talk to me about. If I am right, I am going to need a few people to come with me to talk with them."

"Who do you need, Wren?" Tarek asked.

"You, Leon, and all the shapeshifters. Oh, and Silke."

Tarek laughed, "Don't you mean you want us all to come with you?"

Wren looked around the circle and laughed with him, "I guess I do, most of you anyway."

Pointing at Ted, who was looking longingly at the cabin and probably thinking of the warm bunks inside, Wren added, "Would you stay with Leon and watch over the cabin?"

An audible sigh of relief escaped Ted's lips as he nodded in agreement.

With one last glance at the warm fire, Meg turned to follow everyone to the boat that Tarek had summoned. Once everyone was seated, Tarek flicked his fingers, and the boat moved towards the mouth of the cave. A blast of cold air greeted them at the entrance, but as soon as they passed into the cave's entrance, the air was warmer, causing fog to lift off the water.

At first, Meg wondered why Tarek didn't just warm the water so that wouldn't happen. Then realized that the fog helped to obscure the cave's entrance, and so decided that Tarek knew what he was doing.

Across the boat from her, Tarek laughed and said, "Sometimes."

Meg smiled, and Silke blinked more rapidly a few times before setting off into the cave on her own. Meg knew she was off to visit some of the birds that made their homes in the cave. Meg wondered if the birds thought that Silke was a bird like them, or knew she was a different species altogether.

Suzanne settled herself beside Meg and pulled her closer so that she could cover her with her cloak. Meg knew that Suzanne had always tried to take care of her, but she had never let her. Now she would never be able to repay Suzanne for watching over her.

If Suzanne hadn't tracked her through the portal, she and Roar would have died in the flood that happened after Dax caused the earthquake that destroyed the prison camp.

It didn't take them long to reach where the survivors lived inside the cave. One of the survivors, an older man with no hair and a stooped gait, met them at the front of the ledge that rested over the water.

If he was surprised that so many people had come with Wren, he didn't show it. But as Wren led her band of followers over to the fire, some of the survivors stirred uncomfortably.

Wren lifted her hand and said, "We are not here to change your mind. But I will need their help to do what you are going to ask of me. I thought this would save time."

Most of the group relaxed after that and made room for the arrivals around the fire. But Meg noticed that one man sitting as close to the shadows as possible remained tense with a tiny scowl on his face. She recognized the look. Angry and suspicious. But was it because he was afraid, or because he was going to cause trouble?

Tarek helped Meg to the fire and whispered to her, "Keep an eye on him. You are right. He might be trouble."

Meg wasn't surprised that Tarek always knew what she was thinking. He was a wizard, after all.

That thought only made him laugh again. Meg winced. She was used to being a loner. Once again, Meg felt torn between what she thought she had wanted, and what she now had. Is this what she wanted now? Is this who she now was?

"Only time will tell," Silke whispered in her ear, having swooped into view just a moment before.

Across the fire, the man in the shadows looked at Meg, smirked, and echoed what Silke had just said, "Only time will tell."

A shiver ran up Meg's arms. This time it was not from the cold. It was fear.

Ten

The man smirking at Meg is making a mistake, Tarek thought. The fact that he wanted to stand up for her, and impose a little pain on the man for smirking was disconcerting. That kind of thinking was not like him at all.

What in the world was he thinking letting some man get under his skin like this? First of all, Meg could take care of herself, and second, he might be misreading the man's intention. After all, the man had been imprisoned by Dax for months. That could cause anyone to feel resentment and anger.

Still, he was going to have to find out more about the man sitting in the shadows. There was nothing Tarek could do to stop his feelings for Meg. And as much as his reasoning told him that life would be simpler without being part of her life, his heart knew he had no choice.

The choice he did have was the timing, and Tarek knew that with all that was coming, it was better if they didn't take their relationship too far. Someday when magic was accepted once again in Thamon, and people were free from the spell of Aaron-Lem, they could do more.

Silke laughed in his ear. She didn't need to say anything. Tarek knew what she meant. Good intentions might not carry the day. Feelings for a woman were completely new territory for him. It was not what he had come to the Islands for. He came to make a stand against Aaron and his religion. It seemed like lifetimes ago since he and Leon had decided on this path together.

As cousins, he and Leon had known each other their whole lives. Well, Tarek had known Leon his entire life. Tarek's mom had insisted that the three of them travel to her sister's once she had heard that she was giving birth. They had been there at Leon's arrival.

Looking at Leon sitting across from him now, it was hard to believe that Leon had been so small his father could almost hold him in the palm of his hand.

At first, Tarek had not been interested in Leon at all. He was more interested in practicing his wizarding skills. At the time, his ego had him thinking he would be an even greater wizard than his father, and he worked hard at it every day.

It kept him isolated from the rest of the boys his age, and sometimes even from his family. His parents told him to slow down and make friends. But he didn't listen. He devoted as many hours as possible to magic practice. After reaching a level of wizardry that most people would have thought sufficient, he plateaued. Nothing he did made him any better. In fact, reacting with frustration and anger, he got worse.

His father, the most patient man Tarek had ever met, kept trying to help, but Tarek still wouldn't listen.

Just the thought of that time in his life made Tarek's stomach hurt. Trying to be the best wizard of all time was why he kept failing. The two things didn't go together.

"Unless you sold yourself to the devil," his father would say. Tarek knew that his father would never sell himself to the devil, and through multiple failures and heartaches, Tarek had finally chosen something else for himself. Finally, he had discovered that being the greatest wizard of all time was not what he wanted.

What he wanted was to be a good man like his father, Udore. He wanted to be like the other wizards he met who were protecting their people, quietly and without fanfare. Once that hard-earned wisdom became his guiding life intention, his wizard skills increased, along with his desire to get to know his cousin.

By then, Leon was a young man and surprised that Tarek was no longer ignoring him and treating him like a lesser being because he was an Ordinary and not a Mage.

The families had only visited each other during the warm months. However, the rumors of a coming change in Thamon made them decide to move where they could all be together, and escape together if necessary.

For years nothing happened, but by then, the cousins were the best of friends. They had developed the ability to communicate with each other without speaking. It had started as a game but was now invaluable to their mission.

In many ways, Tarek and Leon were so different no one would think they were related. Tarek was tall and slim with blue eyes and brown hair that curled on his shoulders. Leon grew up to look like his dad, and eventually, he decided to be like his dad and sail the seas.

Leon's mother tried to be happy for him, but she cried and clung to him the day he left. Her husband had left one day in the same way and never returned. No one knew what happened to him, and even though they had all pretended to hold out hope that one day he would return, no one thought that he would.

Tarek didn't want Leon to go either. He had grown used to

having Leon as a companion, and he couldn't imagine what he would do without him. But they promised to keep in touch, and Tarek and his mother and father promised Leon they would make sure their families were safe if the prophecy of danger ever came about.

But more time passed. Leon stayed at sea, and Tarek decided to see the world, too. That was the day that Silke transferred her alliance to Tarek. He didn't want her to. Tarek wanted Silke to stay with his father. But his father and mother insisted, as did Silke, so he gave in to their wishes.

One day the ship he sailed on had stopped at the village where their families lived and he found it burned to the ground. Everyone was gone. The prophecy had come true.

Even though he had been told it would happen, the prophecy had faded into the background of his life. But at that moment, kneeling in the ashes and ruins of his hometown, Tarek's purpose in life became crystal clear to him.

He knew that he had been training his whole life for what he had to do. At that moment, Tarek dedicated his life to stopping Aaron and the men who followed him. The only regret he had was not having stopped him sooner, but he turned that regret into a drive that propelled him forward. He had sent a message to Leon and then set off for The Islands.

Tarek nodded at Leon. They were together again, with the same purpose and same mission. Not just to stop Aaron, but keep the people of Thamon safe, Some of those people sat around the fire waiting for them to tell them if they would be.

Once again, Tarek glanced at the man in the shadows. Instead of ignoring him, he focused his attention on him and wondered to himself, *And what do you want?*

Eleven

The converted were silent waiting for the Seven, also known as the Kai-Via, to enter the Temple, signaling the arrival of the Preacher.

The Preacher was why they were there. His presence and his words swelled their hearts into a feeling of love and companionship. As they waited, they clasped hands and sang. Their voices rang out together in harmony throughout the Temple. No matter how they felt before entering the Temple, they always felt better after only a few minutes of being together within that sacred space.

The one God, Aaron, had decreed new songs for them to sing. But best of all, he had given them a new ritual that allowed them all to have an extra sip from the chalice. Everyone had noticed how much better they felt after that second sip, which is why so many of them came every day for the regular daily services.

It was why there were now two services a day to accommodate the crowds. To keep them from going to both services, their hands were stamped as they entered the Temple so that they couldn't sneak in for both services. Until the hand stamping started, that is what many of them were doing.

Now they had to be content with knowing that they were one of the saved. Still, the people counted the hours until they would be together again with the Preacher and his words.

Anticipation built as they waited. The people knew the Kai-Via needed to look over the room to make sure it was ready for the Preacher's arrival. Most of them had been waiting for over an hour for the daily service to begin. There was never a guarantee that there would be enough room for the service, so to make sure that they were let in, they would line up outside long before the ceremony.

It was freezing outside, but they endured the wait because they knew that inside, with the walls of the Temple closed, they would be warm and safe. They were together in the graces of Aaron-Lem. They were special. They were inside the walls. They were the followers of Aaron-Lem.

At the front of the room, the Seven didn't move. The Kai-Via's stillness and anonymity was always disconcerting. No one could see their faces. Who were they? What were they thinking?

The people tolerated the Seven, which is how it was supposed to be. Aaron and Stryker had designed it that way. They knew that a little fear inspired people to move towards what made them feel good, which in this case was the Preacher preaching Aaron's religion.

It was no mistake that the seven black-cloaked and hooded men lined up behind the Preacher at every service and stared at the crowd. They meant to inspire at least a little fear. Just enough to keep the converted listening to the Preacher, and to not be distracted by other thoughts or ideas.

Although the Preacher also wore a black cloak, and like the Kai-Via, his face was in shadow, he didn't inspire fear. His presence inspired faith and contentment.

Instead of fear, the Preacher gave the people what they

wanted. His words filled their hearts, reminded them that following the tenets of Aaron-Lem would guarantee happiness. Happiness not only for them but for all their families and friends. And they felt that. He made them feel that way.

The Preacher's words reached into their hearts and bound them to him. They believed what he said to their core, or they wouldn't be called the converted. Those that didn't succumb to the message, and could not be converted, were no longer there.

Only when the people weren't at the Temple—after the sips from the chalice wore off and the comforting words faded— did they sometimes notice a slight discomforting tickle in the back of their minds. They would have brief moments of wondering where some of their friends had gone. Where were the unconverted and the Mages that were no longer part of their lives?

During the warm months with the first flush of comfort and hope that Aaron-Lem brought them, and the socialness of their lives keeping them busy, those thoughts had been far and few between for them.

But now, in the cold months, and when the Market where they met in the warm months was closed, they sometimes thought of those friends who used to visit.

But the fear that the Kai-Via had managed to instill in them just by their presence at every service, and sometimes as they walked through the towns, would kick in. They would remind themselves of how happy they had become now that they didn't need to worry or think anymore.

Because of the blessings of Aaron-Lem, they had shelter, food, and a community that met at the Temple every day for the services. Really, what more could they want?

At the front of the room, Dax watched the crowd. As the head of the Kai-Via, he stood with them hidden within his black cloak, his hood pulled even further over his face than usual.

He didn't want to be standing there. He would have preferred to be watching from his hidden room where he could see more. But there had to be seven Kai-Via at the front of the Temple, or the crowd would worry. Only once had they not been there, during the storm and the earthquake. But that had been accepted because of the circumstances.

Otherwise, everything had to remain the same at every service. The regularity of the services was part of the power of it. Everyone knew what to expect. It was comforting to always know what was coming. No thinking was involved.

If something were to change in the daily service, it had to come from a decree from God. From Aaron himself. And Aaron loved to add new rituals, each one carefully designed to add to the comfort and mesmerism of the service. Recently, Aaron had sent new songs, and Dax appreciated not being bored out of his mind hearing the same songs twice a day every day.

But it was that extra sip from the chalice that did the trick to keep the people more subdued over the cold months. It amazed him that Ibris still didn't know that the head of every Kai-Via drugged the water. Dax had learned to do it so well that he wasn't even sure the other six men in the Kai-Via knew about it. The drugged water, both in the chalice and in the conversion pool, was a secret shared only by Aaron, Stryker, and the other heads of the other Kai-Via.

On the other hand, Dax wasn't sure about Ibris. Yes, his preaching was just as mesmerizing as always, maybe even more so. But they had been friends once, and forever cousins, so to

Dax, Ibris' preaching carried a sense of questioning. Dax knew the feeling. He was doing the same.

Twelve

Tarek turned his eyes and attention from the man in the shadows and back to the group. Wren was waiting for Tarek, and once she knew that she had his attention, she spoke.

"Did you vote, or were you waiting for me, Oiseon?" Wren was addressing the older man who had greeted them at the ledge.

He smiled back at her and said, "We voted to have you guide us. We have not yet voted, or chosen, where each of us wants to go."

Wren looked out over the Mages and their families gathered around the fire and tried to keep tears from forming in her eyes. They had been through so much. And why? Because they were not the same? Because they did some things better than other people did? It never failed to astonish her, and dismay her, that people could let themselves be separated in this way.

It was Aaron and his teaching that separated Mages into "the others." For no reason other than he was afraid of them. Not that he would ever admit that. But he was afraid for more reasons than because he wanted all the power, which was probably reason enough.

But there was more, and Wren knew what it was. Perhaps

the time was coming when she would have to share how she knew Aaron and Stryker when they were young. How she knew there was a third man that most people didn't know about.

Wren had watched the three of them become bullies. When they made up their religion so that they could have all the power in the world, it did not surprise her. It scared her. She knew how powerful they were when they were just boys back in school together.

Years of plotting and planning made them more powerful. Now they ruled the world. People bowed to Aaron three times a day. She had heard the rumors about what he did with his staff, The Blessed Ones. A flame of anger rose inside her, but she subdued it—for now. Today was not the day for wrath, but for taking care of these people who needed her.

At the right time, they would deal with Aaron, Stryker, Sawdi, and the minions of Aaron-Lem from the Kai-Via to the Preachers.

All those thoughts went through her mind as she waited for Oiseon to tell her what he wanted. She knew. But it was best if people asked for what they wanted, without her thinking she knew before they told her. Sure, sometimes she did. But she had been wrong in the past. With serious consequences. That couldn't happen again, so now she waited.

Oiseon stood and looked at each person sitting around the fire that was under his care and said, "I'm an old man, but I plan to stay and help the rebellion. But I understand that many of you need to leave and take care of your families. There is no one left for me, so I think the best thing I can do is stay.

"Since I am staying, I need someone that is leaving, to take care of you as you travel. If I have a choice, I'd like to ask Gelon Morgan."

Oiseon turned to look at a young man sitting with his arm

around his wife. Their daughter was sitting on his lap.

Oiseon nodded at Gelon and then looked back to Wren and asked, "If that is okay with you."

"Oiseon, we have known each other for a long time, haven't we? I have always accepted your wisdom, and I believe these people in your care have accepted it too," Wren said. "But are you sure that you don't want to leave? No one would fault you for going.

"Once Aaron, Stryker, and Dax know that you are still alive, they will come after you. And if you are captured, prison camp will feel like a resort."

"I will never be captured, Wren," Oiseon said.

Everyone in the cave knew what Oiseon meant. More than a few tears were falling. Oiseon was loved.

Wren turned her attention to Gelon, who had been whispering with his wife. "Gelon, are you willing?"

Gelon answered her while looking at Oiseon.

"Yes. If I can be half the man that Oiseon has been for us, I will feel as if I have done my part."

Wren looked at each person sitting around the fire. She took the time to look into the faces and eyes of each person, including the children. Finally, Wren turned her attention to the man sitting in the shadows. They stared at each other, until finally he spoke.

"Okay, you win, Wren. You've always been the stronger one. I will stay and fight. That's what I came for after all. And for you, of course."

A long moment passed as the group looked at the man, and then back to Wren, waiting for what Wren would say.

Finally, Wren sighed. "I have never been yours, Karn. So if you came for me, that is a battle you will never win. However, if you want to stay and fight, you have to agree to do it as part of the team. Whatever is decided will not be up to you. Or me, for that matter."

The man in the shadows nodded and lowered his gaze.

By then, Ruth and Roar were standing on each side of Wren, and she looked at them gratefully. She knew they would have been perfectly willing to eliminate the man if he had challenged her further. It was not what Wren wanted, but she was grateful that they knew her, and that they also knew who the man was. It made what she had to do easier.

Turning away from the man, she said, "Now that we have the leader for each group, would the people staying here with Oiseon raise their hand?" Only a few hands went up.

She smiled at them and said, "That means the rest of you will be traveling with Gelon. Where you will be going is someplace that only Leon and Tarek know. And you won't know where you are going until you get there. It's safer that way."

As the people arranged themselves into the different groups, Meg glanced over at her sister, Suzanne. As newcomers to Thamon, they knew nothing about the history of the people. They didn't know how Aaron had managed to make himself the one true God, so they were both surprised continuously at what they learned.

But this time, they weren't the only ones surprised by the conversation between Wren and the man in the shadows.

Suzanne leaned over and whispered to Meg, "Do you know who that man is?"

Meg shook her head no.

It was Silke who whispered back, "I do. It's Wren's husband."

Thirteen

Once the messenger managed to tell Sawdi that Aaron wanted him, Sawdi did what he knew Aaron had meant for him to do. He ended the messenger's suffering. After dragging him into the woods for the animals to dispose of, Sawdi returned to his cabin and gathered a few things that he would need on his trip.

Sawdi muttered as he packed. It was probably a bad habit, but it helped him keep his thoughts in line. His need for order and quiet was offended that Aaron had wasted time by sending him the messenger. He could have sent one of his birds to deliver the message instead.

But Sawdi knew that Aaron loved to visibly use his power in every way that he could, and he took pleasure in setting people up to fail.

Probably Aaron wanted to eliminate the man anyway and thought that Sawdi would enjoy doing it for him.

That was where Aaron was wrong. Sawdi didn't get pleasure from killing people. The fact that he was good at it, and knew how to train others to do so, didn't mean he liked it. Sawdi didn't feel either pleasure or pain at the act of killing. When it was necessary, he did it. Nothing more.

On the other hand, he did feel excited about going to Aaron's Palace because he knew it would involve violence of some kind. *I may like the killing part, after all,* Sawdi muttered to himself. If so, it was essential to know. Knowing oneself was a quality that Sawdi drilled into every one of the Warrior Monks that he trained.

That thought made Sawdi almost snort in pleasure. It was delicious. The name. Warrior Monks. He, Aaron, and Stryker had made up the name one night after drinking too much mead together. It had been a good night. They were brainstorming about taking over the world. At the time, Aaron and Stryker thought it was just for fun. Sawdi was serious.

The three of them had become best pals and drinking buddies after his parents had dropped him off at the school and never came back.

Sawdi didn't blame his parents. He was a terror to live with, and they were frightened continuously by what he did. Not just what he did to others, but often to his parents. As he got older and bigger, they became more and more frightened. They tried to help him but eventually realized it was a losing battle. Sawdi didn't want help. He liked who he was becoming. Actually, he loved it.

The best thing his parents ever did for him was to take him to that school because it was there that he found others like him. With their help, he had blossomed into something he would have never become on his own.

It was ironic that the school was supposed to help them become good citizens of Thamon but instead provided a place for all those sadistic boys to find each other. It was a breeding ground for the people just like him.

Stryker and Aaron were already friends by the time Sawdi showed up. The first thing they did was test his character before they let him into their pack. A lesser man or boy would have folded or died, as many had. But Sawdi survived and thrived under their abuse, finding his own power in response to their attacks. Once they realized that they had found another kindred spirit, they welcomed him with open arms.

The two of them liked being visible. Sawdi did not. He knew that real power was in being the man behind the scenes, teaching and controlling. When in a drunken haze, they came up with the idea of Warrior Monks, the rest of what they wanted to do fell into place. The name itself was perfect.

Weren't monks supposed to be quiet and helpful, praying for the good of the people? There were already religions in Thamon, so the people knew about monks. But a warrior monk, what would they do?

"Perhaps be a hidden army for a new religion," Sawdi had said. With those words, their path forward was fixed. Yes, why not? They could pull the best ideas from each of the religions of Thamon and blend them into a new one.

Warrior Monks were the perfect starting place. If they had Warrior Monks, then they also needed more monk-like people. After many more nights of planning, they decided on the name Kai-Via. Seven anonymous men who could also blend into cultures without being known for who they were. The Kai-Via were the first line of enforcers.

And of course, they needed preachers. The Preachers had to be skilled at using words to convince people that Aaron-Lem was what they wanted. All three knew that in spite of their affinity for inflicting violence, it was words that would make them rulers of the world. Without the perfect words delivered correctly, no amount of force would work.

All of it had worked so well Sawdi had retired to his cabin, believing that his training days were over. But with the messenger's arrival, he knew he was back in business. And as he muttered, he knew he was happy about it. Or what passed as happiness for him.

Grabbing the last few things he wanted to take with him, Sawdi closed the cabin door firmly behind him. As he walked away, he turned back to take a last look. Even from a few yards away, the cabin was barely visible. Behind the cabin, the vultures had gathered.

He wondered if he would ever come back. He did not doubt that if Aaron was asking for him now, it was because Aaron thought that the Warrior Monks were needed again. However, first, Sawdi needed to hear what Aaron thought he wanted. Then Sawdi would direct Aaron to do what he wanted him to do instead. The way he always had.

Halfway down the mountain, Sawdi paused and waited. Within a few minutes, a dragon landed beside him. Patting his massive head, he swung himself up and over. Yes, dragons were outlawed and shot on sight on Thamon as he had directed Aaron to decree.

But not the crown of dragons under his bidding. They remained safe, as long as they served him.

As the dragon rose to take him to Aaron, Sawdi wondered if he should train the Warrior Monks to use the dragons. It was a thought. Sawdi added it to the ideas that he had already started to form.

Yes, he was back, and it was going to be delightful!

Fourteen

While Sawdi made his way to Aaron's Palace, the Mages in the cave were preparing for their journey. Sawdi could safely travel on one of his dragons, but the Mages had to travel using more traditional means, and they would be in constant danger.

Using magic was out of the question. If someone noticed them, they had to appear to be part of the converted community. But all that paled before the biggest problem. Travel, other than designated forms of trade, was now forbidden on Thamon.

Aaron had decreed that where people lived was where they would stay. Tarek knew that Aaron had made that law because he was well aware that travelers spread ideas. The last thing that Aaron wanted was ideas to spread that he couldn't control. New ideas would bring rebellion.

To ensure that never happened, all roads and ships were monitored using spies that reported back to Aaron. These were not spies that Aaron had trained. They were regular people doing what they thought was right—turning in their friends and family when they disobeyed the law.

The fear of being betrayed by a friend or relative was deeply embedded within the tenants of Aaron-Lem. Not overtly, of course.

Instead, the Preachers talked of loyalty. Of taking care of the ones they loved. Of not letting their friends or family stray from the tenets of Aaron-Lem because they would be damned forever, having forsaken the one true God. The Preachers told the people that if you loved your family and friends, you needed to keep them safe within Aaron-Lem.

Thinking about how Aaron controlled people through fear and called it love, infuriated Tarek. He hated that Aaron was using the essential goodness of most people to bind them so profoundly that they turned their friends and family over to the local Kai-Via. They did it thinking it would save their friends and family from destruction in a hell of their own making.

What really happened is they ended up in prison camps like the one that had existed on Hetale until they destroyed it. Even then, ending up in a prison camp was the better option because there was a chance of escape. The other scenario was more final.

Often the Kai-Via didn't want to waste time and resources on unbelievers and eliminated them in the easiest way possible. Whatever was handy at the moment. Drowning, fire, hanging, beatings were only a few of the methods used.

One of the many things that worried Tarek was what would happen if they succeeded in stopping Aaron. What would the people do when released from the hold that Aaron-Lem had on them. What would they feel like? How would they behave?

Would they choose to stay where they felt safe and didn't need to think for themselves? That would split Thamon into factions that fought each other, with or without Aaron. The damage Aaron and his religion had done might never be undone.

Separation and hate could become part of the culture, and the Mages might remain on the unwanted list for many generations. The root of evil ran deep. Could they eliminate it entirely?

Tarek sighed and turned his attention back to the two groups gathering around the fire in the cave. He didn't know what would happen in the long term. But right now, they had things to do. They needed to get the Mages to the safe place that his and Leon's people had prepared for times like this.

Once they were safe, he and the rest of the rebels would have their hands full. The question was, did Leon have to go with Gelon to make sure they traveled safely?

And then there was Karn Kobe, Wren's husband. Seriously? Where had he come from? Had he been in the prison camp the whole time and Wren hadn't told them? Or maybe she didn't known then.

But she hadn't mentioned him after the Mages settled into the cave. So if Karn hadn't been in the prison camp or the cave, where had he been? Was he a friend or foe? All questions that needed answers.

But the priority was getting the Mages and their families to safety. And that meant not letting anyone he wasn't sure of know where they were going, or what they were doing, and that included Karn.

****

Wren knew that she would have to deal with Karn. Tarek was fretting over it.

Actually, everyone was, except Ruth and Roar, because they knew her story. And apparently, so did Silke. How Silke knew was a mystery, one Wren knew she would uncover sooner or later.

Wren thought that she had kept the secret better than that. She hadn't told anyone other than Ruth and Roar about a husband, because as far as she was concerned, he was no longer part of her life.

She hadn't seen Karn for so long she had almost forgotten that he existed. Almost. She had worked hard at not remembering. He had left her so long ago she had let him fade away until he was just a shadow of the past.

Then she saw the man in the shadows smirking at Meg, and she knew her past had come back to haunt her. What she didn't know was why.

Fifteen

Stryker stroked the pendant hidden beneath his shirt. He allowed himself to touch it when he was alone, but he knew it was a bad habit. Someday he would do it when the wrong person was looking, like Aaron. Or, even worse, that freak Sawdi Frey.

Stryker wasn't stupid. He knew that Aaron would call Sawdi back out of retirement. It wouldn't be enough to rule the world through his religion, Aaron would want more. When that happened, Stryker was in trouble, because Sawdi never missed anything.

Stryker knew that retirement was not something that Sawdi knew how to do. Holed up in that cabin, Sawdi was probably plotting and planning something and was waiting for Aaron to call him back to work.

Then all hell would break loose. Aaron and Sawdi would bring the Warrior Monks out of retirement, and unleash them back into the world. The Warrior Monks were Sawdi's plaything, and he loved to turn them on people just for the thrill of it.

Not that Sawdi ever showed his feelings. Stryker just figured Sawdi had to get some pleasure from it.

When they were kids at school, Sawdi loved to manipulate

everyone and was so successful at it most people thought that they were doing things because they wanted to. Sometimes they recovered from what they had done.

However, most of the time, they succumbed to Sawdi's wishes and never thought for themselves again. Sawdi would then turn all the praise and adoration towards Aaron, preferring to remain in the shadows.

It was Sawdi who suggested to Aaron that Stryker be put in charge of the conversion process. Stryker didn't think that Aaron was aware of what Sawdi had been doing, but he was, and the power that Sawdi wielded made Stryker nervous. It was one reason why finding all of the pieces of the pendant was a priority for him.

He needed to have more power than Aaron and Sawdi. First, because it would be safer that way, but also because he wanted it more than he desired food or sleep or any material thing. All he wanted was the power to be, or do, anything he wanted at any time.

Ever since he had found the top third of the pendant, he had been on high alert, waiting for someone to come to take it away from him.

If the Mages, shapeshifters, and wizard hadn't died in the prison-camp flood, he would be worried about them. For a while, he did worry that maybe some of them lived, and would try to take the pendant back before he found any more of it.

But there had been no hint of magic on the Islands. All he had to worry about was Aaron and Sawdi and after he found the whole pendant, he would be safe. In the meantime, he would work with his two old friends. Their plans were his plans after all, because eventually he would take over all of it.

In the meantime, in the absence of resistance from the Mages, Ibris' preaching had become even more popular, if that was possible. So many people wanted to convert to Aaron-Lem they had to increase the conversion ceremonies to three times a week.

The power of Aaron-Lem had spread throughout the Islands, and the people kept demanding more. With no one around to stop it, the Islands were entirely under the spell of Aaron-Lem.

Watching every person on the Islands stop three times a day and bow towards Aaron was thrilling. They had done it. They had made Aaron-Lem the only ruling power, and soon they would begin to use that power to build even more riches for themselves.

The conversion was only the first step in the plan. The next step would be starting soon unless something stopped it, which was only possible if there was still magic on Thamon. Well, there was. But it belonged to the three of them.

With all that at stake, Stryker had to make sure no one was hiding on the Islands that would come after him, or take the pendant away and hide it again. He had sent Falcon to search out any Mages or shapeshifters that might have escaped and were hiding somewhere.

Falcon had returned, saying that all was quiet. There was a small group of Ordinaries living in a cabin out by a lake, but other than the fact they were so far away from the town, there was nothing unusual about them. Stryker didn't like that they were there, though. They were harder to contain. Once the weather warmed up, he would send a few Kai-Via to bring them back into town where he could keep an eye on them.

That left only one person on the Islands that he had to worry about: his prodigy, Dax. It bothered him that he had to worry about him. After all, he had handpicked and trained Dax and Ibris to be precisely who they appeared to be. Ibris calmed the people, Dax kept them in line.

But Stryker was still worried. Stryker knew that Dax was hiding that he was angry. Dax had wanted to keep the Mages in the prison camp alive because it gave his men something to do. Then Stryker demanded that they destroy the camp, and Dax had followed those orders.

However, now that the Islands were tame, Dax would be looking for something to do. Besides, Stryker thought that Dax knew about the pendant. He had caught him staring where he hid it as if he could see through his cloak and shirt.

The pendant didn't look like anything spectacular. It was just a flat gold piece hanging on a chain. It was missing the middle part where the ruby sat, and the last third which would hold all three pieces together. When he found those two pieces and snapped them into place, he would be the most powerful person on the planet.

No one would want him to have it, which meant he couldn't trust anyone.

Stryker pulled the map out of its hiding place and unrolled it looking for answers to where to find the next piece. But the map continued to elude him. It never looked the same.

Sometimes it mocked him by showing him only a blank page. On those times, he would panic, thinking that somehow it had been found and been replaced with a regular piece of paper.

Then the map would flash something, assuring him that the pendant was still safe, but that was it. Stryker knew that when it was the right time, it would give him more information. But right now, he would love to know if the next piece was on the Islands or somewhere else. He unrolled the map to see if today was the day that the map would give him more information. But there was nothing.

It was another day of waiting and worrying.

Stryker knew that time was running out. It was only a

matter of time before Aaron would send someone to check on him, especially if Sawdi was back at work and paying attention.

The three of them were too close not to know what the others were thinking. As hard as he worked to keep his thoughts concealed, he knew that sooner or later, Aaron would know, and then so would Sawdi.

Or maybe it was the other way around. Either way, he would be in big trouble.

Sixteen

An apparent stroke of luck helped with the first part of the plan to get the Mages and their families off the Island. Eos, the ship that had first brought Leon and his men to the Islands had returned a few days before on its regular supply schedule.

When Silke asked Captain Lira if he would be willing to take the Mages back with them, he only paused for a moment.

He and his men had seen the destruction all over Thamon. They sailed the seas, trying to stay out of trouble while trying to contain their anger and despair at what had happened to Thamon.

On the ship, they were reasonably safe. All ships and their crews were needed to keep supplies flowing. Lira had paused only because although his crew had been together for a long time, he knew that there was always the possibility someone would turn them in to save themselves, or their families, from Stryker's punishment for harboring Mages.

Captain Lira didn't believe that would happen, but knowing it could stopped him for a moment, but not enough to say no to refugees.

He and his crew had brought Leon and his men to the Islands hoping that they would make a difference in stopping the spread of Aaron-Lem. And although he had not noticed any difference yet, he had faith that they would succeed someday.

When they told Lira that three of Leon's men would travel with the refugees, he was delighted. The crew had been doing what they could with their limited cooking skills, not having found anyone else to cook for them since Leon and his men had left the ship. The captain knew that all of Leon's men knew how to cook.

The thought that they would be eating well again made his mouth water. Plus, the men and the refugees would bring with them some of the food they gathered during the summer months and had kept fresh in the coldest part of the cave.

Leon had volunteered to lead the refugees, but Tarek had said no. He needed Leon with him. The two of them decided Vald would be one of the men who would leave. Vald's feet should be fully healed by the time the ship landed on their homeland, and besides, there was always the danger that Dax would recognize him if he stayed.

Once the ship arrived, they would need people that could lead the refugees to safety, and fight if it was needed, so they asked for more volunteers from Leon's men. Ted and his brother volunteered to leave with Vald. That left Leon with five of his men to help with the rebellion on the Islands. It would have to be enough.

Since getting the Mages to the ship had to be done without magic, Silke and Tarek couldn't transport them the way they had from the prison camp. That meant walking in the cold and at night. Silke, Leon, and Tarek would lead them.

But Meg also asked to go, and so did Suzanne, Wren, Ruth, and Roar. They were going as support and would not travel as Mages. Meg couldn't anyway, even if they were allowed to. The dark still robbed her of her ability to shapeshift.

Tarek thought too many of them were going, but he couldn't stop them. The support team used the excuse that not all the Mages had fully recovered, and besides, some children had to be carried. "And we need to bring food," Meg reminded Tarek.

Finally, he had agreed that it was a wise decision. They would need help getting through the woods, and the extra support would make a big difference.

Once the decision had been made, they decided to leave the next night. Everyone helped prepare them for the trip, including the Mages that were staying.

Even Karn helped, but Tarek wondered if that was because he knew he was under constant surveillance by everyone who loved Wren and wanted to make sure she was safe, and not because he was a good guy.

Once they got back from taking the refuges to the ship, Tarek planned to have a long talk with Wren about the man she said was her husband.

However, Karn would not be part of the group walking to the ship, so Tarek spoke with Oiseon about what to watch for while they were gone. Four of Leon's remaining crew would stay in the cave, leaving one of them, a man named Fionn Boid, in the cabin so that it wouldn't look deserted in case Stryker's Falcon came back.

The Falcon worried Tarek. It was Wren who had seen the Falcon and knew whose it was. She watched as it circled overhead and then turned back to Hetale. No one was worried about what it saw that time, because Wren had blocked what the Falcon had seen. So, for now, they were safe.

But they knew that once the warmer months returned, Stryker would send people to the cabin to bring them back to either the city of Woald or Tiwa to keep an eye on them.

The plans were to move to Woald by then. But they knew

that their disappearance would alert Stryker to the possibility that a rebellion was in the works. That made it imperative to get the people off the islands and to safety before all that began.

Tarek insisted that the Mages and the families who would be traveling get as much rest as possible. Once they started walking, there would be very little time for rest, and the warmth of the cave would be a distant memory. Most of the families agreed, but the families where some of them would be staying behind spent the day talking.

Tarek couldn't blame them. Hopefully, they would see each other again, but it was possible these would be their final moments together.

As darkness fell, they helped the refuges into the boats and brought them to the shore of the lake outside the cave. For most of them, it was the first time they had been outside since being rescued from the prison camp a few months before. They breathed in the crisp cold air and turned around and around again, enjoying the last of the suns' rays glancing off the lake.

Meg stood with them, holding the hands of two of the young girls traveling with their parents. Tears ran down Meg's face as she took in the beauty of what they were seeing.

Meg tried to stop the tears, but they kept on coming. She had spent years not feeling anything. Now it seemed to her that all those feelings were taking over without her consent. She certainly had not consented to be Ordinary during most of the day. She wasn't even sure she could shapeshift anymore because they had been forbidden by Tarek and Silke to use magic of any kind.

Now instead of magic, she had tears. At the moment, she felt it was a poor substitute.

Seventeen

Two regular services a day and three conversion ceremonies a week were getting to him. Ibris was exhausted. It started with the drain of holding everyone's attention. After every service, he had nothing left. He poured all of himself into the words, spoken and unspoken, into the waiting minds of the people in the Temple.

In the past, he had time to recover. But that time kept shrinking as Stryker and Dax kept adding services to his day. Neither of them understood what that meant to him. They didn't have to convert minds.

If people rebelled or questioned, Stryker and Dax used physical force, which only gave them more energy. The idea that being with people drained him was not something that they understood, or wanted to understand. Why would they? That would mean they would have to stop and think about something other than what they wanted.

However, Ibris knew that something was going on with Dax. And that something could either be a good thing or a bad thing. That thought drained him too. Could he deal with whatever Dax was going to tell him? Because he was reasonably sure he knew what was troubling Dax.

Something Dax had learned but thought that Ibris didn't know. The decision to speak or not speak within Dax's mind was so loud that sometimes Ibris felt like putting his hands over his ears to stop himself from hearing it.

But that wouldn't work. It was his ability to read the thoughts of others that made him good with using words to manipulate people. However, the ability to read everyone's thoughts was not something anyone knew he had, except for his parents. But they were long gone. So he was alone.

However, it wasn't just the ability to read the thoughts of others that he hid. It was that he felt them too. It was the feelings and emotions of people that tore him apart every day.

And every day, he had to put himself back together and pretend that everything was the same. Pretend that his body was not betraying him. Pretend to himself that he was not betraying Aaron by not revealing that he was not Ordinary. Those betrayals were terrible enough. Those factors were out of his hands. He hadn't chosen them. They chose him.

It was the things that he had chosen already and the ones that he was thinking about choosing that were the problem. And it was getting worse.

Lying on his bed, waiting for the next service, Ibris prayed. But not to Aaron. He prayed to the God he had grown up with. The unknowable God who held the world and the universe in her hands. The God that provided all light. That God. The God he was supposed to have left behind when Stryker had rescued him and Dax.

And he had. For a long time, he had pushed the God they called Ophy away. Even more than that, he had denied what he had inherited from his mother. Magic. At first, he had done it out of gratitude for Stryker.

That decision had saved him because if Stryker had found

out about what else he could do, he knew what would have happened to him. He had seen it happen to others. He had gone along with betraying the God his parents had given him, and choosing Aaron-Lem, because he thought Stryker and Aaron had saved him.

What Dax was going to tell him, Ibris already knew. He knew that it had been Stryker who had raided their towns, killed the people, destroyed their homes and villages, and then pretended to rescue the two of them because he wanted them for his own purpose.

Yes, Ibris knew that already. It was that discovery that had brought him to the Islands. It was what made him convince Stryker to convert the people of the Islands peacefully. He was trying to make up for all the damage he had already done.

He knew where the next battle would be. And he knew what side he was going to have to choose. But until Dax said out loud what he wanted to tell him, he could continue to pretend that he didn't know. He could hide away in the Temple, converting people to the false God that Aaron, Stryker, and Sawdi had made up.

And it was Sawdi that Ibris was afraid of because it was Sawdi who controlled the Warrior Monks. If there was any hint of a rebellion anywhere, it was the Warrior Monks who would arrive to control it. So far, Stryker believed that Ibris had peacefully converted the Islands, that Dax had destroyed all of the resistance. But Ibris knew that wasn't true.

He had watched the wizard and his friends rescue the Mages from the prison-camp. It had been the same day that Stryker had found the top half of the pendant. He had seen both because he had been there, watching.

The ability to transport himself anywhere was another gift from his parents Another gift he hid. He had only used it that night out of desperation. He hadn't had to reveal himself as he had feared, but he had seen all that happened. Including the dragon swooping in to rescue the two people drowning in the flood. A dragon. Not one of Sawdi's dragons. He had no idea where it had come from because all the dragons except the ones under Sawdi's control had been killed.

And yet, there it had been swooping out of the sky and then flying towards Woald. That meant that the Mages and their rescuers had to be somewhere on Lopel. They were careful about using their magic, but wherever they were, Ibris knew they wouldn't wait forever before they began their rebellion. What form it would take, Ibris didn't know. He just knew that at that point, he would have to make the choice he had been dreading.

He would have to choose to betray the people he had worked so hard to convert in order to rescue them. He would be hated and hunted. But there was also a glimmer of hope because he would not be alone anymore. That is, if the rebels believed him. Otherwise, he would be an outcast and once again on his own. He added to his prayers that he would be accepted.

Eighteen

The eight of them hid in the bushes and watched the ship, Eos, sail away. The bushes were like the ones where Tarek had waited for Leon and his men to come ashore just a few short months before. But that had been on Hetale. This time the ship docked in a harbor on Lopel because it was safer.

So much had changed, and yet so little. But getting the group of Mages and their families on the boat was a victory, and in their quiet way, they were celebrating it.

Making it across Lopel in the dark had not been easy, but no one complained as they tripped over logs, and wild rose bushes scratched their arms and legs. It had taken them all night to get to the ocean. Just as Etar's pale blue light peeked above the horizon, the last person stepped into the boat that transported them to the ship.

Tarek had gone on board with the first group to make sure everyone was comfortable. He and Gelon confirmed with the crew that they were happy to take the refugees to safety.

Once Tarek was assured that all was well and that Gelon would keep them safe, Tarek returned to shore on the last boat. But before he left, Tarek thanked Lira for what he was doing and what he had done when he brought Leon and his men to the Islands.

Lira slapped Tarek on the back and said, "We will get them to safety. And we are counting on you to stop Aaron and Stryker."

Tarek assured him that they would, and they would see him again soon. But as the eight of them watched from the bushes, Tarek thought about what the captain didn't know. It wasn't only Aaron and Stryker. They also had to stop the man Sawdi Frey. What he knew about Sawdi was something he was going to have to share with everyone once they got back to the cave. It would not be a joyful conversation.

But something else bothered him. He knew that even if they succeeded at stopping those three men, Aaron-Lem would continue. Some people would never let it go because they believed that it gave them what they wanted.

And in fighting for people's freedom, it had to include their right to choose what and who they wanted to believe in. But it would be the first time that the people of Thamon would divide themselves into factions.

Before Aaron's meddling, the people were happy to let everyone believe what they wanted and worship whichever god that they chose.

Tarek doubted that the die-hard converts to Aaron-Lem would be willing for that to be true. Returning the people to the peaceful harmony they had once enjoyed, would take more than stopping the rule of three men who controlled Aaron-Lem now. What that would be, Tarek didn't know. He only prayed there was something, and they would discover it in time.

The eight of them stayed in the bushes, watching the ship become a small dot on the horizon. They were going to wait in the bushes until nightfall, once again being cautious in case someone was watching them. But still, no one complained.

Instead, they lay on the cold ground smiling. Meg moved closer to Tarek, and he wrapped his arm around her to keep her warm. Silke snuggled between the two of them and fell asleep.

Ruth and Roar did the same thing. They pulled close together, and Roar let his cloak fall over the two of them. Tarek smiled at the picture. The two of them, old friends who took care of each other.

Leon sat alone, looking as if he had lost his best friend. But when Tarek looked over at him, he managed a smile. He missed the three men, but he had to trust that he would see them again.

Suzanne and Wren sat together, Wren's head on Suzanne's shoulder. Tarek knew that the two of them were the strength of their small group. Suzanne was the big sister for everyone, and Wren was the leader just as the group of Mages had known her to be.

As Trin rose, Tarek did something that he had told everyone else not to do. He used a little magic to warm the ground and spread the bushes over the eight of them so that even a Falcon flying overhead would not see them. It was a simple reward to celebrate what they had done together.

Meg stirred in her sleep, and Suzanne glanced over to see if she was okay. It was what Suzanne had been doing her whole life, and she couldn't help it. Tarek loved her for it, and he knew that Suzanne loved him for caring for her sister.

Meg's continuous transformation had surprised them both. Suzanne watched as Meg, the wild child who never thought of anyone but herself, cried as the children she had been taking care of left with their parents. Tarek couldn't believe that he, someone who never wanted a relationship, had fallen for this woman who had come to Thamon.

Both Suzanne and Tarek knew that Meg was doing her best not to show her fear that perhaps she would eventually lose all her shapeshifter abilities. And they admired her for it. She was putting the bigger tragedy on Thamon over her smaller one.

To both Tarek and Suzanne, it was a small miracle. Another reason to smile and celebrate.

Wren watched the two of them and smiled to herself. She knew what was going on with Meg, and she knew what Meg's choices would end up doing for her. If she continued down the path she was going, it would be a good thing.

What wasn't good was who was waiting back at the cave. Wren was happy about the delay in returning. It gave her more time to decide how much to tell everyone about her once-upon-a-time relationship with Karn. She would also have to explain how Karn got to the cave. He had put them at risk because he had probably used magic. No one was going to be happy with him once they found out.

All she could hope was that he had done it for the right reasons. But in the past, doing things for the right reason was not Karn's strong suit.

Still, watching Meg sleeping in Tarek's arms gave her hope. Meg was changing. Maybe Karn could do the same thing.

Nineteen

Returning to the cave should have been easier for the eight of them. They weren't carrying supplies or holding the young ones who had gotten too tired to walk. It was a clear night, and although Thamon didn't have any moons to light their way, the stars were bright.

Meg thought that two suns didn't make up for not having a moon. She missed it. Sometimes the moon on Erda had been so bright it was like looking at a spotlight. Other times it hung low on the horizon, looking like a huge orange ball suspended in the sky.

Meg's favorite was when the moon looked like a silver boat in the sky, and she would pretend that people were floating across the night sky inside of the moon.

Now Etar's pale presence was the closest she would get to that moon. Etar's blue light reminded Meg of twilight on Erda. But it wasn't the same.

The seasons were different too. Erda had four of them, each one special. Thamon seemed to have only two. The warm months and the cold and dark months.

Meg hoped that over time, her homesickness for Erda would fade, and she would enjoy all that Thamon had to offer instead of taking it for granted the way she had with Erda. She had been so busy making trouble and doing whatever she wanted to do, she hadn't appreciated what she had.

She certainly hadn't appreciated her ability to morph into any living thing at will. She had made fun of her sister Suzanne because she could only be one thing, a dragon. A magnificent one, but still just a dragon. Meg could choose to be anything, and she had never failed to lord that over everyone she could.

Being banished from Erda had changed everything.

Now she was Ordinary much of the day. No magic. Even if Tarek had allowed her to use it, she couldn't shapeshift when it was dark. And she wasn't sure if she could shapeshift to anything she wanted to anymore. What good would she be to the rebels?

Even though Meg was learning that Ordinary didn't mean useless, or without gifts that could be used to do many things—like Leon and his men—she couldn't let go of the fear that she would be nothing without her magic.

In spite of all that, at least a few good things had come from her banishment to Thamon. Watching Tarek make his way effortlessly through the dark woods was one of those things. She could barely see him, but she knew what he looked like. It was burned into her brain.

Whenever she got a chance and thought he wasn't looking, she would sneak peeks at him. His blue eyes were always so serious, and when he turned them on her, she felt herself melt. Not something that she ever thought would happen to her.

Well, nothing that was going on was anything she had ever envisioned happening to her. Meg wondered what would happen next. Whatever it was, she knew it would not be anything that she would ever have expected.

****

As they stood on the hill that looked over the lake and cabin, Etar's last rays lit up their surroundings enough to see that there was no smoke coming from the cabin's chimney. Trin had set a few hours before.

"Wasn't someone supposed to stay in the cabin while we were gone?" Suzanne asked.

She didn't expect an answer. They all knew that something was wrong.

"Let me go check," Leon said. "If the Falcon saw me before, it would expect to see me again. Maybe Fionn fell asleep and let the fire go out. You are supposed to be dead, don't give yourselves away yet."

Both Tarek and Wren nodded in agreement, but as Leon started down the hill, Silke darted forward and hid in his cloak. It was heavy enough that her pulsing light was invisible.

Leon strolled out of the woods, down the hill, and across the open expanse to the cabin, as if he didn't have a care in the world. He wanted anyone watching to think he was returning from a walk or out hunting for food. He had stopped and picked a few mushrooms on the way out of the woods to help that illusion.

Tarek knew that Leon was anything but nonchalant. He could see telltale tension across his back and knew that fear and anger were burning inside that calm exterior.

"Do you see anything?" Tarek asked Leon.

"Not yet," Leon pushed back into Tarek's mind. "But I don't hear anything either. Fionn should have heard me coming by now. I'm making enough noise to wake the dead."

Realizing what he just said, Leon said, "Ziffer. If something happened to Fionn, I'll kill whoever hurt him."

Tarek looked over at Meg, Suzanne, Ruth, and Roar

crouched low to the ground, waiting for him to tell them what was happening. He shook his head at them, and they all turned their attention back to watching Leon.

As Leon got closer to the cabin, he started walking faster and calling out for Fionn. When there was still no answer, he ran to the door and pushed it open so hard it slammed against the far wall.

The cabin was dark, cold, and empty. Everything looked normal, the same way it had looked when they had left. Except the fire was out. When Leon touched the ashes, they were cold. It had been at least a day since Fionn had been there.

Silke was checking every corner of the cabin while Leon stood and watched, not believing what he was seeing. Fionn would never just leave. Either someone took him or whatever happened was so fast he didn't have time to leave a note.

Leon felt like screaming or sobbing but did neither. He just stood in the center of the cabin, not having any idea of what to do next.

It was Silke who told him what to do.

"Pretend as if this is nothing, Leon. Light a fire. I'll tell Tarek to take everyone around the lake to the cave. You and I will go there tonight. But for now, we have to act as if this is what you expected. Just in case someone is watching."

Leon nodded, happy to be told what to do. They would meet everyone in the cave after dark. In the meantime, he would act as if he expected Fionn to be gone. If someone were watching, he would make sure they only saw a man returning home. Nothing more.

Twenty

One of the Blessed Ones whispered in his ear that Sawdi had arrived. Aaron smiled to himself. He knew Sawdi would come. Sawdi was probably grateful for the chance to do something again. How he could stand to live in that horrid cabin on the mountain was a mystery.

Aaron's eyes swept around his throne room. It was beyond beautiful. It was stunning. He had filled it with treasures that he had his men take from all around the world as they converted the people to Aaron-Lem.

Although he had filled every room of his Palace with treasures, this room was where he lavished his attention. If he got bored, there was more treasure to choose from in the massive storehouse he had built under the Palace.

He was wealthy beyond measure, and his throne room contained as much evidence of his wealth as he could display in one place.

Etar and Trin's light streamed onto the floor through the stained glass floor-to-ceiling windows he had built specifically for this room. This room where he commanded the world.

Even now, Aaron's breath would catch in his throat as he looked around at what he had built. It was glorious. It far

exceeded his wildest boyhood dreams. He had wanted the room
to impress and intimidate anyone that saw it, and he knew that
he had succeeded.

The room displayed every element of wealth he owned.
Nothing was subtle. Gemstones mined across Thamon were
set into the walls. They swirled and marched across the walls
in various patterns making the walls look like tapestries. Every
once in a while, a large diamond was set into the mix. When the
light was just right, the diamonds would send rainbows of color
across the white marble floor to blend with the colors already
there reflected from the windows.

The platform where his throne sat was also polished
white marble. But it was his chair that he cherished. It was
a masterpiece, carved out of one tree trunk, polished to
perfection, and designed to fit him perfectly. Its simple elegance
was deliberate. The room was a jewel box. He was the God in
the middle of it. A simple God. The God who loved nature, as
his tree chair clearly stated.

Another of Aaron's favorites were the curtains that hung
to the side of every window. Each panel had taken months to
weave. Made of spun gold woven so loosely, they looked like
gold spider webs. As weak as the sun's rays were at this time of
year, they still lit up the strains of gold, making the curtains look
like rivers of light.

Aaron knew that the room was gaudy and over the top. That
was precisely what he wanted. He loved to watch people stop
and gawk at it. It never failed. Even if they had been in the room
before, they would still be stunned each time.

The changing season, the placement of the sun, all turned
the room into a different jewel box. It was never the same. It
was always mesmerizing, which is what he wanted. The room's
immense wealth and changing elaborate beauty kept his visitors

distracted and easier to control.

It was too bad the Blessed Ones couldn't see what the room looked like. But no one could look at a God and live, and he didn't want always to be hiding behind a cloak as he was when he met with visitors.

Visitors were different than his spies. People who worked for him were either permanently blinded, like the Blessed Ones, or blindfolded. He did not need to impress his spies with his wealth. They worked for him. Fear worked better.

It was the visitors that he wanted to impress. They saw the room. They never saw him. He hid behind his cloaks. Unlike the Preacher's and Kai-Via's cloaks, which were always black, his were bejeweled and feathered, as befitting a God, except when he wanted to hide. Then he used the plain black ones everyone used.

The cloaks were a brilliant strategy. It kept them all anonymous. There was power in anonymity. He could walk among the people, and they never knew it was him. It made him the best spy of all. There was no middle man to hide or spin the story.

He knew who was betraying him in the local villages and towns. But in the rest of the Thamon, he needed spies, unless he wanted to travel, which he didn't. No place would be as comfortable as his Palace. He would if it was absolutely necessary. He didn't think it would be. Sawdi should insure that for him.

Visitors were essential to Aaron. He invited people to his throne room, who he wanted to help him keep his people under control. Not all of the spying and enforcing was done by Preachers and Kai-Via. He needed more to spy for him. He wanted his visitors to return home and do as he asked them to do. He needed them to spread stories about the glory of Aaron.

The one true God. Him. And he needed his visitors to convince others to spy on each other.

The wealth of the room and the fear of God didn't always work. So sometimes those visitors never returned home. He reduced them to a pile of ashes with the flick of his wrist.

Then the Blessed Ones were called in to sweep up the ashes, and he would spend a moment or two pretending to mourn for their passing. It was their fault they died, not his. If they would only have chosen differently, they would have lived.

Today was a special day. Sawdi was returning to the Palace. The most important visitor of all. Although Sawdi had been to the Palace a few months ago at Aaron's request, he hadn't stayed. Sawdi had told Aaron that Stryker would be crazy to betray him, that Aaron's spies must be mistaken.

This time Aaron knew that he wasn't mistaken. He had more information. But not just about Stryker. There was a chance that a rebellion was forming on the Islands where he had sent his best Preacher and most trusted Kai-Via. Was Stryker part of that rebellion or just unaware of it? That was what he needed to know. It was why he needed Sawdi.

Aaron stepped up to his throne, ready for Sawdi. He couldn't wait for Sawdi to see the changes he had made in the room. Perhaps this time, Sawdi would be impressed.

But then Sawdi never showed what he was thinking. Aaron tried not to care that Sawdi never seemed impressed, and reminded himself that he only needed Sawdi to stay and help him with his plans.

More plans than stopping the possible rebellion on the Islands. Aaron had something else on his mind. He had decided that it was time to start collecting from the people.

Up until now, Aaron-Lem had provided for them. Now it was time for him to collect. Sawdi's Warrior Monks were the answer. They would quell the rebellion and collect from the people what was owed to their God.

The people's free ride was over.

Twenty-One

Ruth and Roar said they would stay in the woods and watch the cabin. After a short discussion, Tarek agreed. He would send someone back with food once they found out what was going on in the cave.

Wren wanted to stay, but she knew that the people in the cave expected her to return and tell them what to do. Yes, it would seem as if the natural leader would be Tarek, because he was a wizard. But it was because he was a wizard that they wouldn't choose him. Wizards were often loners. He might help them and then move on. She would stay.

Tarek was the first wizard that Wren had immediately liked. A wizard's seeming inability to stay in one place made her distrust them. She knew it was irrational. Still, it was how she felt.

It had surprised her and worried her at the same time that she liked Tarek. It could be dangerous. However, so far, Tarek had shown no desire to go anywhere, and that in itself was amazing. Then there was the fact he recognized and supported her as the leader instead of trying to take over.

Part of her wished that he would. Sometimes she would like to be a follower, but it didn't appear to be her lot in life. Long ago, she had stopped complaining to the gods that she was always asked to lead. Complaining hadn't changed anything.

One day she gave up and decided to follow the little voice inside her that told her what to do. Most of the time, she had listened.

Then she had fallen for Karn. What voice had she been listening to about him? Even now, she wasn't sure. Had it been a good or bad decision?

Wren put those thoughts out of her head. There wasn't time for them now. Right now, they needed to find Fionn. Dealing with Karn would have to wait.

****

Tarek tried not to have any expectations of what they would find when they reached the cave. But even if he had, it wouldn't have been what they found. Nothing.

The cave was completely empty. There was no sign that anyone had ever been there. The people had vanished from the cave the same way that Fionn has disappeared from the cabin.

****

Ibris didn't know if he should laugh or cry. After agonizing over what to do, in the end, he had no choice. At least if he was going to be able to live with himself.

He had done it. He had officially betrayed Aaron. He was the Preacher, and yet he had set himself on the side of the rebels. But what else could he do? He couldn't let Stryker find the Mages. The question was, what should he do now?

The only thing he had going for him at that moment was none of them knew who he was. Or at least he hoped that no one knew.

He had to decide what to do with these people before more time passed. At least he had been smart enough to temporarily blind them so they wouldn't know that they were in his chambers in the Temple.

But on the other hand, they were all hysterical, thinking their blindness was permanent. It was terrible. However, he couldn't speak to them to tell them it was temporary. They would recognize his voice.

He had to decide what to do. He obviously couldn't leave them in the Temple. Perhaps, he could bring the wizard to them, but then he would have to tell him what he had done, which meant that Tarek would know who he was. Would Tarek trust him? Why should he? Why should anyone trust the head Preacher for Aaron-Lem?

There was no point wishing that it hadn't happened. It did. It was inevitable.

But what Ibris hadn't expected was Dax's involvement. It was Dax who warned him, and Ibris had no idea why he had. Why didn't Dax just let Stryker find the rebels? Instead, Dax told him that Stryker thought there were still Mages alive on the Islands, and he knew where to find them.

"Get them out of there," Dax had said to the shocked Ibris, "but leave me out of it."

Ibris had stared at Dax. "What Mages?" he had asked Dax, pretending that he didn't know what he meant.

Dax just shook his head and repeated, "Get them out of there. Do it now."

Then he had told them where they were. How did Dax know they were there? Why was he trying to save them? Just a few months before, Dax had delighted in thinking he had killed every Mage and their family on the Islands. And now Dax wanted Ibris to save them?

It made no sense, and it was why Ibris had delayed almost too long. And it was why he didn't have a plan what to do with them now. If Dax was betraying him instead of Stryker, he had put them all into more danger than they had been before he moved them. But that hadn't happened.

Stryker had sent Falcon into the cave, having heard a rumor that Mages were hiding there. He decided to check it out instead of waiting for the warm season.

But Ibris had been a step ahead of him. At the last minute, he chose to believe Dax and cleared the cave. As a precaution, he also took the man in the cabin.

After listening in on Stryker's conversation with Falcon, he knew that Stryker had found nothing, and for the moment, believed that it had been a false report.

Ibris had so many questions. Who told Stryker about the people in the cave? Who knew about it and had betrayed them? Why did Dax want to save them? And how did Dax know that Ibris had the power to do so? Did he know how he did it? Either way, Dax knew things about him, and he could have turned him in at any time. Why hadn't he? Whose side was Dax on?

All questions that needed an answer. But for now, Ibris had to get the people out of the Temple before someone discovered them. Since Tarek and his people had returned to the cave, Ibris decided that it was probably the best place for them.

Quietly, he whispered, "I'm sorry."

Within seconds his chambers were empty as if no one had ever been there. Ibris wished he could pretend that it never happened, but it had. Now, what was he going to do?

Twenty-Two

One second there was no one there. The next, the cave was filled with people and all their things.

For a full minute, no one spoke. What the five of them were seeing was so impossible that their minds couldn't comprehend it.

In front of them, returning Mages stared at each other. Had they lost their minds? They could see again. Everything was as it was before. Maybe nothing had happened? Perhaps it was a mass illusion?

Except now, Tarek, Meg, Suzanne, Wren, and Silke were staring at them, looking just as shocked as they felt, and they hadn't been there before. Finally, Oiseon spoke and broke the spell.

"The fire's gone."

Up until that moment, everyone was ready to write off what happened as an illusion, which was strange enough, but Oiseon was right. The fire was gone.

Hidden from everyone, Ibris watched until he was satisfied that no one knew that it was him who had removed them, or knew where he had taken them.

He couldn't do anything about the fire not being there. If he could have, he would have and hoped that everyone would have accepted what happened as an illusion. But, he couldn't transfer fire back and forth and so he had destroyed it when he took everything else. The cave had needed to look as if no one had ever been there.

So Ibris knew that they would figure out that someone had moved them, but there was nothing he could do about that. He sighed in relief. He had pulled it off.

However, there was one small problem. As Ibris withdrew himself from the cave, he saw Tarek look his way. For a split second, it looked as if Tarek saw him. If he did, his secret was out.

On the other hand, Tarek might not know that the man he saw was the Preacher called Ibris. Someday, he would figure it out. When that happened, would Tarek still think of Ibris as an enemy, or would he accept his help? And, would he give it?

Ibris knew he would have to choose again because although the threat of Stryker had passed for the moment, Stryker's suspicions would remain.

And Ibris knew it wasn't just Stryker who thought there were still Mages. Ibris knew that Aaron thought so too. And then there was Sawdi. Sawdi would simply assume that there were and delight in rooting them out. Everyone would suffer because Sawdi wouldn't care if you were magical or that you were in the wrong place at the wrong time. And his Warrior Monks followed his orders without question.

All of those problems were bad enough. But there was something else. Ibris wasn't sure if it made everything better or worse. For sure, it made him more confused because when he rescued the people in the cave, he recognized one of them. Someone who shouldn't have been there. Couldn't have been there. And yet, he was.

Someone he had met when he and Dax were training with Stryker. Another one of Stryker's favorites. Another boy Stryker had been training. He was older now, but Ibris was sure that it was him.

What had happened? What was he doing on the Islands? Who was he betraying? The Mages or Stryker?

He had no answers to any of those questions. All he knew is that one of those men was the boy he used to know as Karn Kobe.

****

The noise was deafening. Everyone started shouting at once. Meg put her hands over her ears, staring at the people yelling at each other, asking what had happened. Wren waited for a beat and then waved her hand across the group, and the noise stopped.

"Okay," Wren said. "Oiseon, tell us what happened."

"Not sure. One minute we were here, waiting for you all to come back, and then we were someplace else. I think that's what happened because I couldn't see anything. At all. I thought I had gone blind for good. Maybe someone else saw something?"

Wren looked around the group. Everyone shook their heads.

"So everyone was blinded?"

Everyone murmured yes. Wren turned to look at Karn and said, "Including you, Karn?"

"Including me," he answered.

Wren turned away from the group and quietly directed her next question to Tarek.

"Do you know what happened?"

"I have an idea and who did it. But I'm not sure. And I don't know why he would. Why did you ask Karn specifically? Who is he, besides being your past, or is it still, husband?"

"I will answer that question, Tarek. But for now, what should we do? Keep them here or move them?"

Suzanne spoke. "These are the people who want to help with the rebellion, aren't they? Perhaps it's time to treat them as part of the team. Perhaps its time for us to stop trying to take care of them, and let them in on the plan?"

"Do you all agree?" Wren asked. When everyone nodded yes, she turned back to Tarek.

"Could you explain what you think happened, and then we could return to the cabin so that I can tell you all in private about Karn?

"And I would like to send Leon to town to get Samis. If we are going to plan a rebellion, we will need his team too."

Wren turned back to the waiting group, keeping her eyes away from Karn, and then gestured at Tarek to speak.

Tarek looked at the men and women who had stayed. There were eleven of them. Six men and five women. Everyone else, including all the children, had been sent to safety.

All of them were considered Mages. All of them had been in the prison camp and had needed time to recoup. But Wren was right. They had been sheltering these people long enough. Tarek didn't know what skills any of these people had or what they could do.

Finally, he spoke. "I don't know anything for sure. But whoever took you did it because they were trying to protect you. And it had to be because Stryker thought you were here.

"How did Stryker know that? I don't know. But since he didn't find anything, I think you are safe here for now. However, if Stryker suspects that some of you are still alive, he will come back.

"For tonight, Oiseon could you make sure everyone is fine?

We will be back tomorrow."

Tarek turned to look at Wren. She nodded, and he turned back to the group and added, "Karn, would you come with us?"

Karn didn't look surprised. He knew it was coming. What he wasn't sure is what he would tell them—the truth, or something else. It depended. He had an idea who had removed them, and if it was true, it could change all his plans.

No matter what, he was looking forward to spending the night with Wren, even if it was with a bunch of other people who didn't like him. It was something.

Twenty-Three

What had he done? And why?

Dax moaned and dropped his head into his hands. Whatever possessed him to tell Ibris that Stryker was going to find the Mages in the cave?

Now he had problems he had no idea how to solve. He had betrayed everyone on both sides. For what?

Yes, he had finally realized that although he had destroyed the prison camp, those ziffering shapeshifters had saved the prisoners. It had taken him a long time to acknowledge that had happened. He had needed many signs before he could admit that he had failed.

First, there had been that man, Vald. When he came back to his torture room, there should have been Vald's dead body. But he wasn't there.

Dax had written it off because he couldn't figure out how that happened. No one knew about the room. It was hidden behind doors that no one could see through and were always locked. The missing body troubled him, but there was nothing he could do about it without alerting everyone to his secret room. He changed the lock on the door and started looking around for who might know.

He found no one. For fun, though, he had tortured a few people that were acting strangely and then discarded them. But no one had known about the room.

Finally, he decided that he must have left the door open, and someone had retrieved the body to bury it. That wasn't good, but it didn't mean much to him.

However, when he overheard Stryker's Falcon report that he had found a cabin out by a lake, and a few men were living there, Dax panicked. At the time, Stryker hadn't been worried, but Dax's heart had seized. What if one of those men was that Vald guy and he hadn't died?

Those thoughts and fears had Dax examining every part of the day he had killed Vald. After killing him, he had dragged Vald's shapeshifter friend to the prison camp and left him there as he destroyed it.

Yes, he had seen the three Ravens fly overhead that day, and yes, he knew they were shapeshifters. But Dax thought he had destroyed them in the explosion, too.

Slowly a question formed in Dax's thinking, *what if none of that happened?* What if they had created that illusion, and he had been their pawn instead of the other way around?

Over time, Dax had to admit to himself that it was possible. It was then that he went searching for any magic still happening on the Islands. There was nothing. But that hadn't stopped Dax from believing that they were still out there.

Stryker's policy of people spying on each other had eventually paid off. One of the converted reported to Dax that a friend of his had seen a dragon on the day of the explosion. It had been carrying something over to Lopel.

His friend had thought that he might have dreamed it. But the two of them started wondering if it was real. The converted had been afraid to tell Dax about it but thought it was his duty to report what his friend had seen.

Dax had assured them that the dragon was only a dream, and never to speak of it again. Because if he rumors about a dragon, they would both pay the price.

After that, Dax was sure that the Mages were hiding somewhere. He believed that there was a dragon on the Islands that did not belong to the crown controlled by Sawdi. Dax doubled his efforts to find the Mages. In the end, he found them in a totally unexpected way.

One day, he was out walking. Not as Dax, head of the Kai-Via, but as an ordinary citizen. It was something he often did. Partly to keep a pulse on what was happening on the Islands, and partly to get away from the stifling atmosphere of the Temple and all those converted that kept thronging it.

He had never thought he would reach the point that he hated what they were doing. But he did. First of all, the Islands had become so peaceful it was driving him crazy. He liked action. Something to do. Someone to conquer. Instead, Ibris only had to speak, and people practically tripped over their feet to do whatever he suggested.

At least he was honest enough to admit that yes, he, Dax, was jealous of Ibris. But not so much that he hated him. They both had been lied to by Stryker about what had happened to their homes and families.

Dax snickered to himself. Stryker. He had once looked up to him and wanted to be just like him. Not anymore. These days, Stryker was busy with his map, trying to get it to talk to him. Dax had begun to think of Stryker as an idiot. Didn't Stryker know that he, and probably Ibris, and possibly others, knew about the ziffering map and the pendant he was trying to piece together?

Stryker would put the map away after staring at it for hours, thinking no one had seen him. But of course, Dax had. Part of his job was to spy on people, and he was good at it.

Dax knew what it would mean if Stryker found the other two parts of the pendant. He would be in control of Thamon with only his thoughts. He wouldn't need any of them. Everyone knew the myth of the pendant. If it were true, they were all in trouble.

Dax sighed again. He knew why he had told Ibris about the Mages hiding in the cave. The ones he had found because he had followed someone. Someone he and Ibris had known when they were young boys. Karn had disappeared one day, and they had assumed that he had died.

But that day, while he was out walking, his old friend appeared out of nowhere, and Dax had followed him. Karn had walked across the Arrow onto Lopel, straight to a cave hidden on the far side of the Island.

It didn't take a smart man to know who was inside. And Dax was reasonably sure that Karn Kobe knew he was being followed and had led Dax there on purpose.

Dax put it all together and then decided that he would not give Stryker the pleasure of finding out that he had not succeeded at killing the Mages. If anyone were to tell, it would be him, but not right now.

His only choice was to get help from Ibris. But in doing so, he would let Ibris know that he knew that Ibris had been hiding what he could do. It was a chance he decided to take because if he needed someone on his side in his fight against Stryker, it would have to be Ibris.

Besides, it gave him a hold over Ibris. He had let him know that he knew that Ibris was willing to betray Aaron-Lem. Yes, it gave Ibris a hold over him, too, but he couldn't use it unless he revealed himself first. And he knew that Ibris wouldn't do that.

He would protect Dax.

They were cousins who had once been as close as brothers. Maybe they would be again. The question was, would they talk about Karn? Or wait and see what their old friend was up to first.

Whose side was Karn on? Why was he on the Islands? And how did he know where to find the Mages?

Twenty-Four

"Whose side are you on, Karn?"

Karn tilted his head and looked at the woman asking him the question. Her friends surrounded her, but Wren didn't need them to be powerful. Karn was well aware of what his wife could do. He hadn't seen her for so many years he thought that she might have forgotten him. But she hadn't. The trouble was, she appeared to be remembering all the bad years.

He had never forgotten the good ones. Every day he would let himself relive them, if only for a few minutes. It had kept him going as he ran from place to place trying to escape, but his thoughts and memories had followed him.

Yes, what had happened had been his fault. He knew it. It was why he ran. Then Aaron and Stryker and the freak Sawdi took over Thamon, and he couldn't hide any longer. He had to make it right. Even if Wren never forgave him, he had to do it so he could live with himself.

So it was easy to answer Wren truthfully. "Yours," he said.

Wren looked around the cabin at her friends and wondered if they believed him. She wasn't sure if she ever could, but perhaps they had too much history.

They had returned to the cabin, leaving Fionn in the cave

with Oiseon. Fionn wanted to compare his experience with everyone else's who had disappeared. He thought that they might come up with some ideas as to what happened. Maybe they could figure out where they had been taken and who had done it.

The trip to the cabin was quiet. No one knew what to say. They were exhausted and confused. They collected Ruth and Roar, had some food prepared by Leon, gave the three of them a brief rundown on what had occurred, and then settled in to try and figure out what was going on.

Now they were all waiting to hear what Karn had to say for himself. They all also wanted to know the Karn and Wren story. Ruth and Roar knew some of it, but only enough to not think much of Karn.

Karn sat on the floor and let them all stare at him. He didn't think he was anything special to look at. Although Karn usually hid behind a facade of arrogance, he let that drop away so they could see the real him. Or at least as close as he could get to it. The habit of hiding behind a sneer was long ingrained.

Tarek glanced over at Wren, and she said, "He's all yours." So it was Tarek that asked the next question.

"Okay, Karn. You have a lot to tell us. You can either tell us in your own way, or we can ask you questions. Which way do you want to go?"

"Ask your questions," Karn said.

Meg stepped in, "How did you get here?"

Karn lowered his head, dark curls falling forward, and then lifted his head to stare at Wren. He wanted to lie. Telling the whole truth was going to get him into more trouble. But he had promised himself to make it up to Wren.

She sat there looking almost as he remembered. She still looked like a young woman, almost a girl. She was slight and small so she could get away with it, but he knew she kept that look to disarm people. They wouldn't know how powerful a woman, a Mage, and shapeshifter she was until she wanted them to know.

Wren stared back, not flinching. Her steel-gray eyes unblinking.

"I knew Wren was here. I followed her because I wanted to help. I knew she would be fighting against what is happening on Thamon, and I thought perhaps I could make up for my mistakes of the past."

"Okay, nice," Meg answered. "And I am sure there is a story there that we want to know. But that didn't answer my question. We want to know how you got here. Did you come on a boat? When? Where have you been? How did you find the cave? How did you get into the cave without anyone knowing?"

Suzanne smiled at Meg. It was good to see her sister take control. This was where her fearlessness could be used, instead of behaving like a spoiled brat. Perhaps Meg was the answer to finding out about Karn.

Meg understood transformation. She was going through it herself. Perhaps she would be the best person to determine if Karn's change was real or fake.

Karn smiled at Meg too. Not a sneer, a real smile. Here was someone who might understand. Meg did not smile back.

"No, I didn't come on a ship. I flew. It took me a long time. I had to stop to rest and eat. I'm not used to flying such long distances. Besides, I knew that if the wrong people saw me, I would be shot out of the sky."

Karn turned to look at Suzanne. "I recognize what you are, do you recognize what I am?"

Suzanne nodded and turned to Wren to confirm what she thought, "He's a dragon, too?"

Karn didn't wait for Wren to answer. He wanted to save her from trying to explain.

"Yes. Only a dragon, though. That's all I am. So I flew here. Hid on Hetale until I got an idea of what was going on. I've been here a while. Mostly hiding in the woods, and living in caves as I spied on the Kai-Via and the Preacher."

"You were watching your old friends?" Wren spat at him.

All eyes turned to Wren and then to Karn.

"Old friends?" Tarek asked.

"Yes. I used to know the head of the Kai-Via on this island and the Preacher. Long ago. We trained together with Stryker. I was training to be a Preacher like Ibris, your Preacher. But then something happened."

No one spoke. They waited.

"I didn't know I was a shapeshifter. One day, training with Stryker on my own, I turned into a dragon. I am not sure which one of us was the most scared. But I was a boy, and he was the warrior. Guess who won."

Twenty-Five

Karn glanced at Wren, who turned her head away, and Karn looked back at the group and said, "Stryker did what he had to do. As you well know, Mages, especially shapeshifters, are banned in Thamon. What made it worse was I was training to be a Preacher.

"I was so shocked at what had happened to me that Stryker's grabbing me and throwing me into one of the prison cells was almost a relief. It gave me time to think about what had happened.

"I spent the first day alternating between hating myself and being terrified that someone would be coming to kill me. Eventually, I realized that since I didn't choose to be a shapeshifter, there was no reason to hate myself. And if I wanted to live, I would have to escape. So when the door opened, I ran.

"And in many ways, I have been running ever since, which is why I am here. I am tired of running, and this seemed like a good place for me to take a stand. My old friends from school are here, my wife is here, and the chance to stop Aaron-Lem is here.

"Let me help. I know Dax and Ibris. They know me. It's because Dax knows me that we escaped from Stryker."

Karn paused and looked around the room. He hated the looks that everyone was giving him. Wren had turned away from him. Her face betrayed how hurt she felt. He hoped that as he told his story, things would change. Karn took a deep breath and continued.

"I didn't think Dax would give Stryker the pleasure of finding out that he had failed. That the Mages still lived. And I was right. Dax went to Ibris and asked for help. And as I figured he would, Ibris did help. He is the one that saved you. But Stryker will be back."

Karn sat back, knowing that he had only scratched the surface of what they wanted to know about him. But once he told them about Dax and Ibris, their attention would be diverted to them, which was a good thing.

Karn wondered if they knew about Sawdi. If not, that would be a revelation. Not one he was looking forward to telling them. But first things first. Get them to trust him enough to help plan the rebellion.

"I see what you are doing," Tarek said. "Only telling us enough to think we can trust you. But I won't believe you until there is proof. In the meantime, you need to clarify what you told us.

"First, what did you mean when you said that it was because Dax knew you that you and the Mages escaped. And second, how did Ibris save them? Are you trying to tell us that Dax and Ibris are willing to betray Stryker?"

Karn smirked. He couldn't help himself, even though he knew that smirking was not winning him any friends.

"Let me answer the second part of that question first. Ibris is much more than he appears, and yes, he has magical skills. He thinks, or thought, that no one knew. But Dax and I did. We just never said anything. And for sure, Ibris was not going to tell. He is well aware of what would happen. He has hidden it well. Although I imagine it was a shock for him to discover that he had magical abilities, just as it was for me to realize that I'm a shapeshifter.

"It was Ibris' mother who was a Mage. Something that Stryker didn't know, or he might not have saved Ibris when he had his troops destroy his village. But his mother kept it a secret too."

"Destroyed his village?" Meg asked.

"Sure, that's how Stryker collected all the men who are now Preachers and Kai-Via. He destroyed villages to get the most promising boys to train in Aaron-Lem. All of us were orphans. All of us thought that Stryker was wonderful for taking care of us. We didn't know.

"I figured that Dax and Ibris had figured it out by now, which is probably one reason why Ibris helped Dax. Ibris has always hated the violent part of Stryker's conversion of people to Aaron-Lem. Most likely, it is why Ibris asked to convert the Islands peacefully. Well, relatively peacefully.

"It's probably killing him to know what he knows and to hide what he is. I think by rescuing everyone in the cave, Ibris has finally admitted to himself that he has to stop Stryker. He knows that Stryker only let him convert the Islands peacefully because it made his search for the pendant easier."

Meg asked, "Pendant?"

"So, not all of you know about it? Does anyone?"

Tarek answered. "I know about it. If the myth about the pendant is true, it makes sense that all Stryker wants to do is get all three parts as quickly as possible. He has one. Are the other two pieces on the Island?

"He wants them to be. Perhaps they are. I think Wren knows." Karn said.

Wren glared at Karn and shook her head at Tarek, so Tarek asked the question everyone needed an immediate answer to.

"We are still waiting for the answer to how Dax knowing you saved the Mages."

"I showed him where they were," Karn answered.

No one said anything. Everyone sat in stunned silence waiting for whatever was going to come next, or for someone to ask the next question, or for Karn to keep talking.

Karn let out a breath that he didn't realize he was holding. He had taken a chance telling them outright like that. But their reactions told him something about everyone in the room. Some people were so angry that they didn't move. Others were more calculated. Karn watched them carefully because he knew that knowing their reactions would give him power.

He could say that he didn't want any power, but they wouldn't believe him. So to get what he wanted, he would need the power of knowing each person well. But no, he didn't want the power. What he wanted was redemption. However, Karn knew that to receive redemption, much would be demanded of him. It didn't matter. He was willing to pay the price.

Even if Wren never took him back, his life would be better than it had been, and perhaps he could help save Thamon. Karn knew that the worst was yet to come. Sawdi would make sure of that.

In the meantime, he had to pretend to be something that he was not. Aaron would be watching. That was something he couldn't tell anyone. Not until they trusted him. Keeping secrets from everyone was not going to be easy, but everything depended on his ability to do it, and do it well.

Twenty-Six

Finally, the map spoke to him again. *Why now?* Stryker wondered. He wished he could control the ziffering thing.

The map had a mind of its own, and nothing he could do would make it tell him what he wanted to know. It worked when it was good and ready.

So many times in these past few months, Stryker had to stop himself from ripping it to shreds or throwing it into the fire in exasperation. It was the knowledge that the map was the only way he would find the rest of the pendant that had stayed his hand.

Sooner or later, he would console himself, *it won't be blank, or show only a slip of information.* If he waited long enough, the map would reveal something to him again.

Ever since he had found the map under the rock on his seventh birthday, he had looked at it every day. He was used to its silences, or habit of showing him only pieces of the world with the rest of the information faded out.

Or it changed what it showed him so that one day he would be looking at a vast expanse of ocean, and another day, the top of a cliff.

But although teasing him had always been the way it

worked, this had been the longest time that the map had ever been entirely silent.

In the past, it had revealed a little information at a time. That's why it had taken him years to interpret the map enough to get to the Islands. However, it had been the intervention of who he believed to be the pendant's creator that had shown him where to find the top third of the pendant. One of the Islands' storms had driven him into a cave, where it had been waiting for him to find it.

Because that was how he saw it. The pendant was waiting for him to find it. It belonged to him.

The storm had proved it to him again. The map had been given to him, not to anyone else. That meant the pendant was meant for him too. He was meant to take over the power to control all the thoughts of everyone on Thamon.

Most people thought that the story of the pendant was a myth. But not Stryker. He knew it was true.

One of the gods that had once ruled Thamon had it made for his son. But the son had abused the power of the pendant. After ignoring multiple warnings from his father that he was to use the pendant's power only for the good of the people, his father took the pendant away, leaving his son powerless.

For years the son searched for the pendant, but his father had broken it apart and hid it, saying that no one would ever have it again.

His son eventually drowned himself in the ocean, and his father, Tewao, the God of the Sky, expressed his grief by periodically sending violent storms across Thamon. And now, Tewao had shown Stryker, only him, where to find the hidden pendant.

Although Stryker knew that the myth was true, some parts of it didn't make sense. If Tewao didn't want anyone to find the pendant, why was there a map?

Perhaps Tewao didn't make the map. And if someone else did, who was it?

Also, why not merely destroy the pendant? Stryker didn't have any answers to those questions, but he did believe the story that the pendant existed and had power. Especially since he had proved its existence. When he found the rest of it, he would control and demonstrate its power.

Stryker knew that he was on the right track. The fact that the storms on the Islands had become more and more violent since he had arrived confirmed it. Tewao was testing him and helping him at the same time.

So Stryker had waited, if not patiently, for the next sign. In the meantime, he tried to pay more attention to what was going on with the converted.

It was his job after all, and if he didn't pay attention, Aaron might get suspicious. Aaron's spies were everywhere. That's why he had acted on the rumor that some of the Mages were still alive. He sent Falcon out to search again.

One rumor was that they were in the area where Falcon had found the cabin. After thoroughly searching the area, Falcon found a cave, which would have made an excellent hiding place, but no one was there.

Stryker had shrugged and written it off as a false rumor, but today when he unrolled the map, it showed him the cave that Falcon had found. That couldn't be a coincidence. Perhaps this was where he would find the next section of the pendant.

The possibility that Mages were on the Islands was not the most important thing on his mind. Perhaps they were, but if he found what he was looking for, it wouldn't matter how many Mages, shapeshifters, and rebels were still alive, he would easily be able to control them all.

Stryker found it ironic that the map, and therefore the inevitability of him having the pendant, had been given to him. Not to a son of a god. No, he wasn't that. But he was a collaborator of a made-up god. Because of what he, Aaron, and Sawdi had done, Stryker thought that perhaps all gods were made up. Stryker laughed to himself. For sure, Aaron was a fake god.

The picture of the cave and its location faded off the map, and Stryker rolled it up and put it in its hiding place. As persnickety as the map was, (and Stryker doubted that it would show anything to anyone except to him), he still needed to be careful about it.

He needed to plan a trip to the cave and find that pendant before it was too late. Before Aaron or anyone else discovered what he was doing.

But first, he needed to have a meeting with Ibris and Dax. They had a problem.

Aaron was implementing the next part of the plan that the three of them had designed years ago. The converted's free ride was over.

Stryker would be responsible for starting the collection process on the Islands. If he didn't do well, Aaron would replace him. For all he knew, his replacement was already on the Islands, just in case he didn't succeed.

Stryker knew Aaron. Friends or not, Aaron wanted it all. Stryker couldn't blame him. He was the same way. That was why finding the pendant was critical before Aaron and Sawdi figured out what he was doing and stopped him.

Twenty-Seven

The rebels made plans to move their base of operations back to town. They would leave Fionn and two more of Leon's men at the cabin so as not to arouse suspicions about where the occupants had gone. Leon's men would also keep watch over the cave in case the rebels needed it again.

Meg watched the group as they decided who would stay at the cabin and who would go to town. Part of her wanted to stay with Fionn. The cabin was warm and safe, at least for now. She figured everyone had a piece of themselves that would like to choose the cabin instead of town, but like her, they were also excited at the prospect of finally doing something.

Silke had asked Samis to find them a place to make their headquarters in Woald. He had chosen another deserted building on the outskirts of Woald, and his small group of rebels was waiting for them there. Even though, thanks to Karn, Dax already knew about the Mages, Tarek still asked everyone to refrain from using magic. There was no need to keep announcing that they existed.

Once again, they would be walking in the dark. Wren would lead the way, and Tarek would follow up to make sure that no one got lost or strayed too far behind.

While she listened to the plans, Meg thought about how many people were now part of the rebels. From the first small core group of Ruth, Wren, Roar, Tarek, Silke, and Meg, the group had grown to include the eleven Mages from the cave, Samis' town rebels, Leon and his men, Suzanne and now Karn.

The size of the group worried Wren and Tarek. How would they control all these people? As the group waited for nightfall, the two of them met outside by the lake to talk about it.

"There are too many people," Wren said. "We were better with just a few of us that we can trust. We should have let all the Mages go on the ship. Even with Oiseon watching over them, we don't know what they can do or how they can help."

"I agree, Wren," Tarek said, "But it's too late now. And we have to move them to keep them safe for now. At some point, we are going to have to take the rebellion to Aaron's Palace. It may be that it will be the Mages who help with overthrowing Aaron."

Tarek paused, wondering how to ask the next question.

Wren saved him from trying to figure it out. "I know you have questions about Karn. I do, too. Is Karn on our side or not? Was having Dax find the Mages so they could be saved really for their benefit, or was it for him? I know you all want to know more about Karn, and I promise to tell you all the story. But for now, the answer is, I don't know if we can believe him.

"We married young. We separated many years ago because I didn't trust him anymore, and Karn got tired of my suspicions and left. I don't know why I would start trusting him now. But watching Meg's transformation has made me believe that it is possible. On the other hand, I don't think we should leave him alone at any point."

"How do you suggest we do that?" Tarek asked.

"Pair him up with Suzanne. They are both dragons, and we

will need them to work together. Plus, ask Leon to keep one of his men watching Karn at all times. At least until we are surer of him."

Tarek smiled at Wren. "Thank you for finding me in the meadow, Wren, and bringing this group together."

Wren smiled back. "You still have secrets, too, Tarek. But then I guess we all do. However, when I saw you, I knew you had been sent to help us, so thank you for saying yes."

The two of them stood together, looking out over the lake, watching the two suns slide low across the sky turning the trees into shadows that sliced across the lake.

As Meg opened the cabin door, ready to tell the two of them that food was ready, she thought that Wren and Tarek looked like a father and daughter standing together. Perhaps they had been in another lifetime. But in this one, they were probably the same age and had come with the same purpose. Release the people of Thamon from Aaron's rule.

Suzanne stepped out of the door to stand beside Meg. Meg turned to look at her sister and reached out to hold her hand. It still amazed Meg that Suzanne had never stopped believing in her.

Suzanne had given up her freedom, family, and friends to find her. In spite of her continuing fear that her shapeshifting abilities were slipping away, Meg knew something had brought them all together. Some force of good that led them to this place and time.

It was a strange thought for her to have. Until coming to Thamon, all she had thought about was her personal freedom. It never occurred to her that anyone else mattered, or that people were tied together by unseen forces, both good and evil.

As Wren and Tarek returned to the cabin, the last rays of Trin disappeared below the horizon, and the world turned dark.

After everyone ate, they would be leaving.

Meg looked up at the dark sky, so unlike the sky from home. Moonless, it was filled with pinpricks of light from star formations she had never seen before. For the first time, Meg wondered if the universe was so vast, and they were so small—how did they matter and to whom?

Were there real gods or a God? Was there something that had led them all to this place to help these people? How could a force so colossal care about them?

It was a question that Meg had never thought about before, but now it filled her heart and brought tears to her eyes. She turned away so that no one would see them, but it felt as if she was shapeshifting in a different way. She was turning into someone else. Was this the trade-off she was making? And if it was, would it be worth it?

Watching her sister and Tarek look at her with love in their eyes made her think that yes, it just might be.

Twenty-Eight

Sawdi's dragon, Bolong, landed outside of Aaron's courtyard, waited for a beat to make sure that Sawdi didn't need him any further, and flew off to hide with the rest of the dragons.

If Sawdi saw him, or any of the other dragons outside their cave when he hadn't summoned them, he would have them punished. And Sawdi's punishment was never subtle.

There were only five of them left. All the other dragons had been destroyed. Dragons were magic, and there could be no magic that the three men did not control.

Yes, Bolong knew about those three men—Aaron, Stryker, and Sawdi. Three men who as boys had terrorized their school, and then grown up to terrorize the world.

They had met Sawdi at Stryker's training camp. After Sawdi turned them into dragons, Aaron recruited them into his secret missions to terrorize the local village.

If they didn't say yes, their lives were hell. So they did what Aaron, directed by Sawdi, asked of them. It was the biggest mistake of their lives because from that moment on, they were Sawdi's prisoners. He wove a spell that kept them as dragons, ready to always do his bidding. The boys they had been were gone forever.

However, Bolong and the rest of his crown were biding their time. Yes, they were only dragons who did Sawdi's bidding, but someday people would rebel, and then they would be ready to join forces to help take back the planet. In the meantime, Bolong did Sawdi's bidding, but with hate in his heart.

Sawdi watched the dragon leave. He had forgotten the boy's name that had grown into that dragon. He only recognized it because of the red streaks in his wings. He liked how easy this dragon was to fly, so he often requested it when he called for a dragon. But Sawdi also could feel the rebellion that simmered beneath the surface. Someday that dragon would turn on him. Sawdi snickered to himself. It wouldn't matter.

While holed away in his cabin, he had been practicing. Every day, his ability to control all forms of life using his mind to focus the energy that existed all around them was increasing.

It surprised him that no one was harnessing that energy except him. Every day that passed, Sawdi improved his skills. Now, along with his ability to manipulate minds, he expanded his ability to manipulate the energy that made up the world. For his own ends, of course.

He would never teach anyone what he knew. It was his power that had made Aaron his puppet. Aaron had always been his puppet. Of course, Aaron didn't see it that way, and Sawdi never wanted him to. There was more power in subtlety and manipulation.

All of Sawdi's suggestions to Aaron about what to do seemed to be something that Aaron wanted. Most of the time, Aaron did quite well on his own, taking over the planet Thamon. Sawdi laughed again. Of course, that desire made Aaron the perfect puppet. He was lost in his need to own and control.

The Palace was the perfect example of the excess that drove Aaron. Sawdi knew that Aaron had probably made the throne room even gaudier than it had been the last time he had been here. Aaron, in his stupidity, thought that Sawdi cared about ostentatious displays of power.

If Aaron had any real awareness, he would only have had to look at Sawdi to see how little he cared about such things. Sawdi wore only one ring on his hand. A small gold ring set with a dark stone. It didn't reflect light. It swallowed it.

Sawdi glanced down at the ring with pride. The ring was his one valuable possession. It was the reason he was the master manipulator that he had become. To make sure it would always be with him, he had placed a spell on the ring so that no one could ever take it off his hand.

As Sawdi walked up the massive steps to the ridiculously enormous front door, a string of Blessed Ones poured out of the small doors on the side. Two men came to his side, ready to accompany him to the throne room.

It never failed to amuse Sawdi that Aaron called these blind people Blessed Ones. Of course, it had been Aaron's idea to promote the fiction that if someone looked at Aaron the God, they would die. That fiction allowed Aaron to do what he did.

Still, Sawdi saw it as an indulgence. How these people made their way around the Palace was impressive. More than once, he had tested one of them to see if they were really blind.

When they didn't step away from the knife he plunged into their shoulders, Sawdi assured himself that they were. He always asked Aaron to send only Blessed Ones with a scar on their shoulder. He knew he could trust them.

Two of the ones with scars walked with him now. He had lost count of how many Blessed Ones he had marked that way. Maybe all of them by now. It made life easier that way.

Aaron waited for Sawdi perched on his throne.

Of course, Sawdi thought. *Arrogant as always.* Sawdi was

always grateful that Aaron had such poor mind-reading abilities. He didn't have to hide his thoughts around Aaron. So he wasn't worried as he gloated over the knowledge that he had made Aaron and Stryker who they were. But the time was coming when he wouldn't need them anymore.

Sawdi was looking at Aaron as he came into the throne room, so he didn't see the small flinch of one of the Blessed Ones walking beside him.

Instead, Sawdi walked up to Aaron's throne and bowed and then accepted Aaron's invitation to move to the small table set by the window. A tea set was already there, and a Blessed One was pouring the tea. By placing one finger at the top of the cup, he could feel the heat and know when to stop pouring.

After the Blessed Ones had retreated, the two of them sat and looked out over the garden. It was beautiful, well managed by many gardeners who were allowed to keep their sight, as were the cooks. But they never had the privilege of being in the same room as Aaron.

"Well done, Aaron," Sawdi said, keeping everything but what he wanted Aaron to believe out of his voice. The two of them sipped their tea, and Aaron listened as Sawdi described what would happen next.

Aaron had no idea that he didn't have any choice in the matter. But even if he had, he wouldn't have cared. What Sawdi told him to do sounded glorious to him, although a small sliver of fear always touched his heart whenever he heard the words Warrior Monks.

But Sawdi always assured him that the Monks were only there to support what Aaron wanted, so it must be true. Aaron decided to be happy with their reemergence. They could help him collect what was owed to him from the people.

Aaron had decided to start on the Islands and see what

happened. It would be an excellent test for Stryker, Dax, and Ibris.

Were they still on his side, or had something changed as his spies had told him?

Sawdi said he would need some time with the Monks. After that, he would take them to Lopel and Hetale. The Islands would make the perfect test case for the rest of Thamon.

Twenty-Nine

It was a strange meeting. Three men in a room. Three men who had to decide how much to trust each other. If at all. But each one of them knew that trouble was coming, and they all wondered if they would be able to handle it on their own.

The three of them were in a small room at the back of the Temple. Another space that Dax had designed into the Temple that was not visible to the public.

It was in that room that all the Kai-Via, Ibris, and Dax would meet once a week to discuss the schedule of conversions, Temple maintenance issues, and news from Aaron.

In those meetings, it was only Dax and Ibris who spoke. The other six men of the Kai-Via listened, nodded, and made mental notes. No written records were allowed in any meeting.

The Kai-Via had all learned to listen well. If they made a mistake during the week because they missed what was said, punishments would incur. Usually, something as simple as no food that day, but it could be worse. What happened to punish the Kai-Via was not something that Ibris knew about. It was Dax who handled all the discipline problems.

In that hidden meeting room, no one wore their robes. That made it easier to see who wasn't paying attention, but it was also the time that they could share and laugh. When appropriate. Usually only when Ibris ran the meeting, if Dax was busy elsewhere.

Today it was only Stryker, Dax, and Ibris who sat together in the room waiting to see who would speak first. Technically it would be Stryker because he was the person in charge, not only on the Islands but as second in command of Aaron-Lem.

But today, Stryker found that he didn't know how to phrase what he needed to say. It had to be perfect. He needed these two men to believe him, support him, and fight beside him if necessary.

He had been their teacher, their mentor, their trainer, and yet he was still worried. None of the three men were friends. They had no loyalty to each other. Stryker knew that Dax and Ibris could turn against him.

Especially since he suspected that they knew he had destroyed villages to get the young boys he had wanted to train. But right now was not the time to turn against each other. He needed them. Until the map revealed the location of the last two pieces of the pendant, he needed them. After that, he didn't.

Dax and Ibris continued to stare at him. Waiting. Stryker had trained them to wait until he spoke. It always gave him the upper hand. Stryker could almost see the two young boys he had first met in the two men that sat across from him now. Almost, but they were no longer innocent.

It was hard to believe that Ibris and Dax were cousins. Dax was dark and low to the ground. When he was angry, his brown eyes would flash gold sparks. Ibris remained calm, almost placid. Ibris could be as still as the Stonenut tree that Stryker knew Ibris loved.

It was hard to read what was going on in those pale blue eyes. Some people had thought that Stryker and Ibris were related because they looked so much alike. Stryker had done his best to quash that idea.

Dax shifted in his chair, getting restless. But with a look from Stryker, he stilled his energy. However, Stryker could see Dax's impatience rising inside, barely contained. It was what made Dax such a good warrior. Now he just had to point him in the direction that he wanted him to go.

Finally, Stryker cleared his throat and said. "I have received a message from Aaron."

Stryker didn't have to speak out loud. The three men had trained in silent communication between their minds, but Stryker didn't like using it. To him, it never carried enough importance.

Stryker knew that Ibris' ability with silent communication was what made him such a powerful Preacher. That was another reason Stryker didn't like using it. He wasn't sure if Ibris was talking to him without his knowledge as he did with the people. So, in their private meetings, he demanded that they speak out loud.

But after delivering his message, both Ibris and Dax remained silent. That, too, was a tactic that he had taught them. He hated that they were using it against him, forcing him to say more, maybe more than he meant to say.

Bowing to their silence, Stryker continued. "We are to begin collecting from the converted. Aaron has declared that he has fed and provided for the people long enough, it's time for them to pay for all that he has given them."

Still silence.

"If we don't collect enough, Sawdi will send his Warrior Monks to help."

Although Ibris did not move, Stryker knew that he was angry. For some reason, Ibris actually loved the people he preached to. Perhaps other Preachers did too, but Stryker knew that Ibris was driven by the desire to make life better for everyone.

Stryker knew that Ibris did not like that they had punished, or killed, the Mages, but had accepted it as a necessity to keep the peace, which is what Ibris desired above anything else.

Now Ibris would have to be part of making their lives worse. Someday, Ibris would reach a breaking point. Stryker hoped it wouldn't be anytime soon. He would hate to have to replace him. But he would if he had to.

When Ibris didn't say anything, and Stryker didn't add any more details, Dax finally spoke up. "And how does he want us to go about this? And what exactly does he want us to collect?"

Stryker looked at Dax burning with anger and wondered if he would have to call in his replacement soon. He didn't want to. He understood Dax.

In fact, he understood both men sitting in front of him. At one time, he might have admitted that he loved them as if they were his sons. But they weren't. And if they got in the way of his quest, he would do what he needed to do.

But right now, they all had to keep Sawdi's Warrior Monks from ever coming to the Islands. Because if the Monks came, all their plans would be over. If Sawdi didn't think the three of them could accomplish what Aaron had asked of them, the Monks would destroy all three of them. Painfully.

Thirty

The building that Samis had found for them smelled as if a thousand animals had died in it. At least that was what it smelled like to Meg.

Samis had smiled and said that yes, it smelled terrible, but it wouldn't take long to get it cleaned. Couldn't one of the Mages just wave their magic wand or something? Tarek had glared at him, and Samis had backed off, but Meg couldn't help but agree.

Just a little magic, please, she thought, knowing it wouldn't do any good to ask. Tarek was adamant about the rule of no magic being practiced. He was sure that Stryker and the Kai-Via were continually monitoring the Islands, and he wasn't going to risk their plans over a smell.

Samis and his small crew had prepared one large room where they could meet, which was reasonably clean and non-smelly. After that, he said that they could divide up into different areas of the building, and as they did so, perhaps they could get rid of whatever was causing the stink.

One thing that Meg was grateful for was that the building was warm. Samis said it was heated by a hot spring that sat below it, making it too hot in the warm months, but perfect for now. It was probably also the cause of some of the unpleasant odor. But Samis promised that they would get used to it. Meg wasn't so sure.

She and Suzanne chose a room right beside the main room with Tarek and Silke next door. Everyone else had found rooms down the various hallways in the building.

It had been many years since Meg and Suzanne had shared a room. Not that Meg remembered liking it, though. She never had a moment to herself. Suzanne was always watching. How things had changed. Now she was grateful that Suzanne was still watching over her.

Wren and Tarek had suggested that everyone get some rest, and they would meet later in the day. Samis and his team would bring food back. The five of them had been in hiding for months in town and knew where they could get food and supplies without anyone seeing them. Since Aaron had instigated the spy-on-your-neighbor-for-their-own-good policy, it had gotten more dangerous for them. But not as dangerous as if one of the others went out.

Before anyone ventured out onto the Islands, they needed a good plan. Meg hoped that someone had one. As far as she could see, all they were doing was gathering a group that did nothing but hide.

She and Suzanne finished cleaning their room the best that they could, and then using the blankets Samis' team had provided, they both lay down on the floor and fell asleep. But not before Suzanne said, "Sweet dreams, Meg," and Meg replied with a catch in her throat, "You too, Suzanne."

Across the hall, Wren and Karn stared at each other in a room so small it was probably once a closet. They were there because neither of them wanted anyone to hear their conversation. But the room was hot and cramped, and neither of them knew what to say.

Wren thought back to when they used to talk all the time. They would discuss everything. It had been secret conversations then too, but joyous ones. They had been foolish thinking that the world that they enjoyed would stay as pleasant as it was forever.

She had been the most foolish. This lifetime was not her first lifetime. She had long ago lost track of how many times she had returned to Thamon. Each time a little wiser, but obviously not wise enough. She had let herself fall in love with a young boy. Yes, she was old. But in this timeline, she was his age and ready to enjoy another life.

Karn's family were friends with her current family, so they were always together. Their days had been filled with roaming the countryside, swimming, and climbing trees. Sometimes friends had joined them, but often they went alone, and over time, both of them knew that someday they would marry.

Karn knew that Wren remembered her lifetimes, and she was a shapeshifter, but it didn't bother him. The division between Ordinaries and Mages was not part of their life, and it never occurred to either of them that someday they might be on different sides.

When distant rumblings of warriors taking over towns and villages became part of their parent's whispered conversations, neither of them had paid any attention. Then one day an army arrived in their town.

Announcements were made in the public square. Aaron, the one true God, was now the ruler of the land. A Preacher arrived along with seven men, called the Kai-Via. They passed a decree. Come to the Temple and be converted, or else.

The or-else is what happened to their town. But Wren had used some of her lifetimes of wisdom and escaped. Karn was captured, and the village was burned to the ground.

The few people that Wren helped escape went into hiding, included both her and Karn's parents. Karn's parents begged her to find their son, and she agreed. Not just for them, but for her, too. He was her best friend.

It took time, but she had eventually found Karn at one of Stryker's training camps. What she saw scared her so much she didn't let him know that she was there. She knew that his reaction to seeing her might give her away, and then they both would be lost. Instead, every day, Wren transformed herself into something else and watched, waiting for the chance to rescue him.

Finally, Stryker left to train at one of the other camps, and she found her chance. But not before Karn had been seen as a dragon and thrown into a cell. She was the one who had opened the door. They had escaped together.

Karn watched Wren, his dark eyes giving nothing away. Wren waited. She had no idea where to begin.

Karn took a deep breath and slowly blew it out. "Wren, did I ever thank you for rescuing me?"

Wren waited a long moment before answering. "No. You didn't. Maybe because you never left what Stryker was teaching you? How do I know what side you are on, Karn? I couldn't tell before. How can I tell now?"

Thirty-One

Bolong waited as Sawdi told him to. He had learned how to behave like an obedient dragon. But while Sawdi was distracted, Bolong had slithered as far away from where Sawdi was standing as possible.

He knew what was coming, and he was terrified. Not only was he afraid because of what Sawdi was getting ready to do, but that sooner or later, Sawdi would not want anyone to know what lived here in this desolate place.

As far as Bolong knew, he was the only one. Not even Aaron or Stryker knew. Yes, sooner or later, Sawdi would want to destroy him. When that time came, Bolong hoped that he was ready.

Knowing what Sawdi was up to, Bolong knew that he had time. Sawdi would need him and the other dragons for a little longer, and even though he hated what Sawdi was doing that would give them that time.

Keeping as low a profile as possible, Bolong watched Sawdi as he stood at the edge of the cliff. They were in a gray, desert-like landscape. Flat, open, with no visible life. The few creatures that lived there would never show themselves while Sawdi was around.

As Bolong waited for Sawdi to do what he came to do, the two suns passed each other low on the horizon. Bolong prayed for a glimpse of the blue flash that would give him hope that Sawdi would not be successful in bringing back what he had put into the canyon.

Instead, the suns passed each other without fanfare and then sank lower on the horizon, making it hard to see anything other than Sawdi on the cliff and his shadow elongated behind him.

Sawdi didn't move. Bolong knew that he didn't have to. His silent call would reach to the bottom of the canyon, passing through the shrubs clinging to life on its side, sliding through the boulders resting at the bottom until it reached the ones below the surface of the hard, dusty ground. There it would be heard by the hundreds of beings waiting in a state of suspension. Waiting to be called into service again.

Watching Sawdi highlighted by the dying rays of the suns, Bolong wondered how many people knew that Sawdi was the real ruler of Thamon. It was his words, his desires, and his plans that Aaron put into action.

Aaron thought that Sawdi was his adviser. It just showed how blinded Aaron was by his greed and lust for power. But Bolong knew about the three boys who masterfully terrorized their school.

A school where every boy was there because they had frightened their friends and family and they were no longer wanted at home. Aaron, Stryker, and Sawdi had gained the upper hand at that school and never let go.

Bolong knew Sawdi was even then in control of the other two. Bolong knew Sawdi chose to not be in the spotlight, allowing—no designing it—so that Aaron and Stryker would be the ones that the boys, even the teachers, and now all of Thamon, feared. Or, in Aaron's case, worshiped.

But Aaron always wanted more. Of course, it was Sawdi's unseen influence that increased Aaron's need. It was easy to manipulate Aaron. He had always wanted more power and more wealth. More jewels to bury in his walls. More Blessed Ones to serve him and then destroy with a flick of the hidden device he wore on his wrist.

But that was not what Sawdi wanted. He had no riches, no jewels, no one waiting on him hand and foot.

Bolong was not sure what drove Sawdi, which was what made him so frightening. He couldn't be figured out. He did what he did following no one's rule or guidance other than his own. *How can someone like that be stopped,* Bolong wondered.

Although Sawdi's wrath, when he chose to exercise it, could be very visible, Sawdi's control over Aaron was subtle. Whispering. Directing through silent signals. Which was what Sawdi was doing now standing on the cliff. Silently calling.

In spite of himself, Bolong trembled. He knew what was coming. He heard them before he saw them. The sound was so low it was barely there, but the pitch of it made his bones ache.

That sound had given him nightmares for years. It was like the low hum of a bumblebee amplified not in a noise level, but in its intensity.

Like the bee, what Sawdi was calling to him, was directed and focused on what the queen bee and the hive wanted and needed. In this case, Sawdi was the queen bee. He made them, and they did his bidding.

Bolong, and anyone who had ever heard that sound and seen what they could do, had hoped that Sawdi would never call for them again.

They relived what they had seen in their survivor's nightmares.

As Bolong watched, they rose above the cliff, swarming.

White wraiths. Barely visible. Humming. Waiting to be directed by Sawdi.

The Warrior Monks had arisen again. Bolong backed as far away from them as possible, making himself look as non-threatening and invisible as he could. If they turned their attention to him, he didn't know if Sawdi would call them off.

One figure separated himself from the swarming mass of wraiths and floated in front of Sawdi. If they said words, Bolong didn't hear them. The leader melted back into the swarm, and then the entire group of them whooshed away.

Sawdi turned to Bolong with a smile. Bolong recognized that smile. He had seen it before as Sawdi had put into action something that hurt someone. Bolong knew what that meant. The Warrior Monks were on their way to someplace to hurt someone. Probably many someones.

As Sawdi climbed onto his back, Bolong saw something he had not noticed before. Sawdi's ring, the one piece of jewelry that Sawdi always wore, was glowing. It faded quickly, and Bolong prayed that Sawdi hadn't noticed that he had seen it.

Thirty-Two

Ibris stood before the converted and conveyed the message that Aaron had sent. He did his best to soften it, to make the people believe that was what they wanted to do. He told them that they were grateful to be given a purpose, a better way to serve the God, Aaron.

For a moment, they had resisted. Then Ibris felt them give way. Sighing. Letting the air escape from their lungs as easily as they were going to release what little wealth they had to Aaron-Lem.

They had time. Aaron, the gracious God that he was, would give time to collect what they owed him. The warm months were almost upon them, which meant they would soon be able to plant the crops that Aaron wanted.

For now, they only had to turn over all the gold and jewels that they owned. Not that the people of the Islands had much gold or gemstones. Wealth like that had never interested them. So Ibris hoped that Aaron would understand that there was not much to give.

Today was the first day that a basket was to be passed around to collect their jewelry and gold. If you had them on while attending the service, you had to take them off and put them into the baskets. The Kai-Via walked through the crowd passing the basket down through the aisles. They gestured with their cloaks flowing over their hands to anyone who hesitated to be quick about it.

These people had no warning that this was going to happen. Ibris watched, his eyes hidden by the hood, as women took off their rings, necklaces, and bracelets and dropped them into the basket. He kept the words flowing, trying to ease the letting go, trying to have them feel warmth at letting go rather than sorrow over what they were losing.

Little did they know how much more they would be losing. But his job was to keep these people safe. At least that was the job he had given himself. Ibris knew that meant he would have to seek out the rebels to get protection for the people. The words he spoke during the ceremonies were not going to keep the people happy forever.

When Aaron demanded half the crops and half the crafts that they used to trade, the people would feel the loss. They would be hungry. Hungry people would not be silenced with his words, no matter how well spoken.

As the Kai-Via turned back to the platform with baskets filled with gold and jewels, Dax caught Ibris' eye. A flash of understanding passed between them. Dax was not happy with this decree, either. His job was to enforce it, and as much as he liked fighting, and making the Mages suffer, he was worried, too.

Dax knew that he and the Kai-Via would not be enough, and as Stryker had said, that meant the Warrior Monks would be sent in. They had heard rumors about them, and all of them were terrifying. Both of them had seen the destruction they left behind.

Before the service was over, Ibris silently impressed upon

the people that they could not share what had happened at this service with anyone. All the people coming to these first services could not know that they would be giving up all their gold and jewels. If the baskets became less full at each service, Stryker would know, and then they would have to go house to house to collect.

Before the Kai-Via, the people of the Islands were always smiling and talking. After Aaron-Lem arrived, the exuberance that people had once felt had faded. But they hadn't noticed. They weren't supposed to notice. Instead, they were quieter and followed the orders given to them both out loud and silently.

However, today was worse. The people all filed out silently, barely looking at each other. Something had been deliberately taken away from them, and it was not just their treasures. Their belief that they were safe had been eroded. Not that they were consciously aware of that fact, but they knew something had changed, and it made them sad.

Sooner or later, Ibris knew that they would have to get mad. They would have to join together to fight Aaron's takeover of their lives. But when they got angry, their anger would not always be directed at the right people. And Ibris knew that he would become the target of some of that anger, and in his heart, he knew that they would be right. Maybe he should have stopped this long ago.

Only the thought that he had no idea how to do it and no one to help him, kept him from going down into a pit of self-hatred. He couldn't afford to do that anyway. He needed to be clear to come up with a plan. He needed to know who to trust and how much. Like Dax. Was Dax going to help or not? If he was, how much should he trust him?

As the people filed out, Ibris scanned the crowd until he saw who he was looking for. The man who came to the services, and pretended to be converted, but Ibris had known for months that he wasn't.

Ibris assumed he was one of the rebels. One of the Ordinaries that his preaching did not affect. The drugs that Dax had secretly slipped into the water didn't seem to affect him either. There had to be more of them. They had to be banding together. He needed to talk to them and the Mages he had rescued and get their help. But first, he had to get them to trust him.

He couldn't call out silently to the man he knew was named Samis because Samis was immune to it. Instead, he went back to his room, slipped out of his cloak, and then followed Samis, hoping he would find a way to talk to him alone.

It was dangerous. Samis was big and much stronger than him. On the other hand, he had magic. Ibris smiled to himself. They all had gifts. If they put them together, there was a chance they could save the Islands, and after that maybe, just maybe, all of Thamon.

They at least had to try.

Thirty-Three

Samis knew that someone was following him. He had seen him in the market place months before the Preacher and the Kai-Via arrived. Or at least that was what they had been told at the time. The official arrival of the Preacher and the Kai-Via had been very public.

Many times during a service, Samis had tried to catch a glimpse of who the Kai-Via and Preacher were behind their dark robes. But it was impossible to tell. Besides, he had to look as if he was one of the converted, and the converted were not curious.

So even now, as he walked, he couldn't appear to be curious or notice that someone was following him. This person could be one of the Kai-Via walking among the crowd as Samis suspected they had done long before they supposedly arrived. It would have been what he would have done. Wasn't he doing that now? Pretending to be something he wasn't.

To make sure he was right, Samis didn't walk in a straight line. He walked up and down streets as if he was out for a stroll. Which in itself was suspicious, and he knew he couldn't do it for long.

It was freezing. A cloud bank had hidden even the little

light and warmth that the suns were giving off, and a wind had come up off the water. He worried that another storm might be brewing.

Given that the storms had become so threatening that it wasn't safe outside, Samis knew that he had to find shelter soon. But then, so did the man that was following him. Because now it was apparent that was what was happening. He couldn't go to the building where the rebels were hiding, so he chose the only thing he could think of to do. He stopped and waited.

At first, the man following him did the same thing. They stared at each other, and then the stranger moved forward. Samis waited, his fists clenched. As the man got closer, Samis could make out blue eyes staring out from under the hood of his cloak. The stranger smiled, and Samis couldn't help himself. He smiled back,

"What do you want," Samis demanded, through his smile.

The stranger replied in a very familiar voice, "I need your help. And I think you need mine."

****

Hidden from view, Karn watched Samis as he waited for the man to catch up with him. He knew that Samis didn't realize that it was Ibris, and he wondered what would happen when they met. Based on Samis' clenched fists, it could be anything.

On the other hand, Ibris was so non-threatening, Samis would probably give him time to talk. Words were Ibris' gift. Samis would probably listen. Then decide.

It had been a long time since Karn had seen Ibris, but he looked much the same. Taller, a little older, but Ibris still had the same quiet stillness that Karn had admired in him back in Stryker's training camp.

Even then, Ibris was ready to stick up for those who couldn't stick up for themselves, including, for a time, himself.

He hadn't done well after Stryker's men had captured him. He missed his parents and the life that he had, and he had mourned Wren, thinking she was dead.

Bitterness and sadness were his constant companion, and it made him vulnerable to the bullies in the camp. The bullies were the ones training to be Kai-Via, and they loved to practice their dominance on those chosen to be something else or the ones who didn't measure up. Karn wasn't sure what happened to them. Knowing Stryker, he was sure it wasn't good.

Even then, Ibris was able to stop bullies without fighting, using words, which made him special in Stryker's eyes. Ibris and Dax. Stryker's favorites. Not him. Although before Wren rescued him, he was being trained to be a preacher like Ibris.

He wouldn't have made a good one. He was more like Dax. Impatient, ready to fight, not trusting. Unlike Ibris, he hadn't seen himself as someone that needed to protect the people. He had been out for himself. That is what Wren had finally seen in him, and in the end, what had caused their separation.

Karn found it ironic that they were all together again. It was as if it had been preordained from the beginning. That's what Wren would say, anyway. Here they all were: Wren, Karn, Stryker, Dax, and Ibris.

Had the Islands called them together? Is that why Wren had come here? Did she know they would all end up here? Did that mean that Wren knew what would happen next?

As the two men stood facing each other, apparently oblivious to Karn's presence, Karn wondered how much Wren knew. On the other hand, maybe she didn't know what would happen because of him.

Perhaps it was up to him to make the right choice on his

own this time. What he did know was that he was going to betray someone. The question was, who would it be? That's what Wren was asking, and he couldn't tell her the answer.

Thirty-Four

Tarek stood in the middle of the room, staring at Silke, hovering in the air in front of him. "I swear I thought you said that Ibris, the Preacher on this Island, Stryker's favorite Preacher, is a wizard."

Silke didn't answer, just waited. Tarek looked around the room at everyone who appeared as shocked as he was and turned back to Silke.

"I think you better tell us how you know that, Silke. I am assuming you wouldn't say such a thing if you weren't sure. And perhaps you can explain how a wizard has managed to live within Aaron-Lem. And how he could allow those terrible things to happen to other people like him. How can he live with himself?"

"I can't," Ibris said, standing in the doorway. "Which is why I'm here. I was going to ask Samis to bring me, but then a storm came up, and Karn decided to rescue us."

"Probably trying to force the issue," Wren muttered.

She looked at Ibris and said, "Sit. You have some explaining to do."

Tarek pointed at the table to have Ibris seated directly opposite him. He wanted to watch Ibris' every move. How had he not known Ibris was a wizard? Silke's people were always paired with a wizard, so perhaps that's how she knew, but why hadn't she told him?

Once everyone was seated, Tarek looked at Wren. "Perhaps you'd better run this meeting, Wren."

Wren smiled back at Tarek. She understood that he wanted to observe. And he wanted to give her a chance to force some answers from Karn.

Karn spoke up before Wren had a chance to ask him anything. Wren recognized that as a control tactic, but she was willing to let him hang himself if that was what he wanted to do. On the other hand, he might tell the truth. Wren wished she knew what Karn was up to. He was always up to something.

"I know Ibris because we were part of Stryker's training camp, along with Dax."

Meg spoke up. "I know that all of you probably know what he is referring to, but Suzanne and I don't. So, if you could add a bit more detail, it would be helpful."

Tarek smiled at Meg. She had changed so much. In spite of losing her ability to shapeshift at night and in the dark—which in this season meant almost all the time—Meg wasn't complaining. Instead, she continued to transform herself from a wild child who didn't care about anyone, to someone he had come to love. Tarek mentally shook his head. He was being distracted, and Silke's snicker in his ear as she sat on his shoulder confirmed that.

Across the table, Tarek saw Ibris shoot a puzzled glance at Meg and Suzanne, and realized that Ibris probably had no idea where they had come from. That was a good thing. Keep him guessing while they figured out his motives. Sensing what Tarek was thinking, both Meg and Suzanne winked at him, and he couldn't help but smile back. Silke snickered again.

Karn had stopped to watch the exchange between the three of them before answering Meg's question. He cleared his throat and said, "Here is a short history. Some of which the rest of you might know, but to put it in context, this is what happened.

"Aaron, Stryker, and another man most of you don't know named Sawdi, ended up in a school for troubled boys together. The school and their contact with each other just increased their aggressiveness and desire to control.

"Bored with controlling the school, they decided to take over the world. They figured that the best way to do that was through a religion. So they designed Aaron-Lem."

Meg nodded. She appreciated this encapsulated version of events and realized that she was not the only one who hadn't heard about the third man.

"Aaron was to be the God of Aaron-Lem. Couldn't help himself, he had to give the religion his name. Stryker was in charge of recruiting young boys to train them into being the visible part of Aaron-Lem—the Preachers and Kai-Via.

"Except he didn't recruit, he stole them. First, he destroyed their homes and families, and then made them think that he rescued them.

"Most of the boys believed him and were grateful for the chance to be trained into something useful. There were many of Stryker's camps set up around Thamon. But Dax, Ibris, and I ended up in the main camp, and were directly taught by Stryker."

Meg interrupted Karn, "So he rescued boys to train them. What about the girls?"

Ibris and Karn exchanged looks, and Karn replied. "Some lived. It might have been better that they didn't. They were given to Aaron."

"For what?" Meg asked.

Tarek turned to Meg, and said, "Meg. This answer might be best to talk about later. I promise we'll get to it at the right time."

Meg looked around the room and realized that no one wanted to talk about it, so she let it go—for now.

Karn continued, "I was at the camp until Wren found me and rescued me."

Karn looked at Wren and said, "Sometimes, she probably wonders why she did it, but I have always been grateful. We have known each other since I was a boy. Wren, as you probably all know, only looks the same age as me. She is lifetimes older. And wiser."

Wren broke in, "Enough of that, Karn. Later. Get on with this part of the story."

"While I was at the camp, it was obvious that Ibris would be a preacher. He was calm and knew how to use words. Dax was impatient and wild, so he trained to be the head of one of the Kai-Via."

This time it was Suzanne that interrupted Karn. "Don't you all find it very odd, perhaps disconcerting, that all of you who knew each other before coming to the Islands?

"And if Meg and I understand what has happened correctly, how in the world did you, Ibris, who we now understand to be a wizard, escape the detection of Stryker and Aaron?"

Once again, Ibris and Karn looked at each other.

Then Ibris said, "Before we tell you how, perhaps, you should know that Stryker, Aaron, and Sawdi use magic in one form or another, some more powerful than the others. But they are what they are banishing and killing in Thamon."

Meg and Suzanne exchanged looks, and Meg knew that Suzanne wished that Meg had never come to Thamon.

What had she gotten the two of them into, Meg thought. It was so much worse than she feared it would be.

Thirty-Five

Bolong dropped Sawdi off at Aaron's castle and then left as quickly as possible. He hated being there. It was the symbol of all that had happened to Thamon.

Besides, he wasn't sure where the Warrior Monks had gone, and he didn't want to be anywhere near them in case they were close by. If they weren't humming, they could appear out of nowhere. He had seen what they could do, and he never wanted to see it again.

As Bolong flew back to where the other four dragons waited, he watched carefully for any sign of the Warrior Monks, but they had vanished.

That was the problem. The Warrior Monks could come and go at will once they were released from the stasis that Sawdi had put them in. Sawdi was the only person who had any control over them because Sawdi was the one who had raised them from the dead, and turned them into wraiths.

Aaron named them Monks because he wanted to have monks as part of Aaron-Lem, and Stryker added the name of Warrior because he loved crushing the people through war. It was an excellent name for spreading fear, and once anyone heard or saw the Warrior Monks, fear is what they felt.

Bolong wondered if Sawdi was ever afraid that his creation would turn on him. Although part of Bolong wished that would happen, he knew that only Sawdi knew how to return them to the hive and keep them there. So if the Warrior Monks turned on Sawdi now, no one on Thamon had a chance.

Until they figured out how to stop them, Sawdi had to stay alive, not just to control the Warrior Monks, but to release Bolong and the rest of the dragons from the spell that Sawdi had placed on them.

Sawdi had frozen their shapeshifting abilities. He had told them that it was forever, but after seeing Sawdi's ring glow, Bolong wondered if perhaps it was the ring that made it possible for Sawdi to do the magic that he did.

There was someone who might know the answer to that question, but he hadn't seen him for years. Somehow he had escaped the boys' camp that Stryker ran. But he had told Bolong that he had discovered a secret about Sawdi. Was that a secret that could save them now? If so, why hadn't he come forward?

Perhaps he has died, Bolong thought. Or he is a prisoner somewhere. Bolong prayed that wasn't so.

However, if Karn was alive and free, he needed to do something soon before it was too late.

****

Sawdi snickered to himself as he watched Bolong return to his friends. It wasn't hard to know what Bolong was thinking.

Someday he would have to kill him, but for now, he loved riding dragons too much to eliminate them—especially ones that belonged to him.

Bolong did an excellent job of bowing and scraping, pretending that he was a loyal servant. However, Sawdi knew that was impossible unless Bolong was a fool, which he wasn't.

It was fun to taunt him, though. Take him to where he had stored the Warrior Monks so that Bolong would know that his days were numbered. Scaring Bolong would keep him under control for a while. He knew what motivated Bolong, and he admired him for it.

It was why he had chosen Bolong and his four friends to be his personal crown of dragons.

Bolong and his friends had been useless at Stryker's camp and he, Aaron, and Stryker had fun pushing them around. But after a while, that wasn't fun anymore.

Sawdi had no idea why Stryker had chosen them to be in that camp. But then not all those boys he stole worked out. If he had feelings, Stryker might have felt sorry for them. All of their families were gone. But Sawdi didn't have feelings, so instead, he thought of different ways to torture them every time he visited the camp.

Stryker was all for letting them be playthings for the more aggressive boys at the school.

But one day, Sawdi had seen the five boys sneak away from the school and had followed them.

Of course, magic was not allowed at the camp. So the five boys must have known that what they were doing would mean punishment.

Part of Sawdi couldn't blame them. They had probably just discovered that they were shapeshifters and were curious about what they could do. He remembered when he had first found that he had some magical abilities. It was intoxicating. And he would often sneak off to practice.

So watching the boys laugh and giggle as they shifted into dragons brought a few moments of pleasure to Sawdi remembering how that felt.

But he couldn't let them have fun. He had to do something. Then it occurred to him what use the boys could be if they were dragons all the time. They could be his private crown of dragons. And as they grew, they could become quite handy weapons if he needed them.

It was Bolong who saw Sawdi first as he stepped out from behind a tree. Bolong's face turned white, and it looked as if he didn't know whether he should run or stay. He stayed.

He stepped in front of his friends and said, "Sorry, sir. It won't happen again."

Sawdi laughed. The boys, thinking that perhaps he wasn't so scary after all, didn't know whether to laugh or not, but tried a smile to see if that was allowed. All except Bolong, who had composed himself and stood, waiting.

He knew that something was going to happen, and there was a chance that he could save his friends from it.

"I'll give you a choice," Sawdi said. It was his voice that made the boys realized that his laughter was at their expense, and not an expression of joy.

"Yes, sir," Bolong had answered for the five of them.

"You can die now, or live as dragons serving me."

The four boys behind Bolong began to cry. Bolong did not. He answered for all of them. They would be dragons. Sawdi knew that in his heart Bolong had decided that one day he would find a way to get back at Sawdi. But if Bolong was dead, he couldn't.

Yes, he knew that there was betrayal in Bolong's heart. Once again, Sawdi understood. He had betrayal in his heart too. But only one of them would win.

Thirty-Six

Tarek leaned back in his chair and looked around the table, wondering who had already known before what Karn had just said about every head of Aaron-Lem having some magical abilities. He thought that perhaps Wren did. Probably, Ibris. Anyone else?

It was Wren who answered what he was thinking. "Yes, I knew. How could I not? I had watched the camp for many months before figuring out a way to rescue Karn."

"Why didn't you tell us, Wren?" Ruth asked. "Roar and I have been your friends for years. We've worked together. When Aaron-Lem came to the Islands, you never told us that you knew who they were. We've trusted you, why didn't you trust us?"

Wren sighed. "I understand that you might wonder if you can trust me now. But I did help you rescue your family, and as many other people as I could. So it wasn't because I didn't trust you. I didn't want to frighten everyone else even more than they were."

"But shouldn't you have told us before we rescued the Mages from the prison camp?" Meg asked.

"Clearly, I don't understand all the manipulations and

decisions that are going on here, but wouldn't we have been safer if we had known that the heads of Aaron-Lem have magical abilities?"

When everyone started talking at once, Tarek raised his hand, and the conversations stopped.

"We can't start doubting each other. What we need is more information, so I suggest we talk without blaming anyone until we hear the whole story.

"I suspect that what Suzanne said played a part in why Wren has kept quiet. There is a reason why we are all here together. Old friends have found each other. Secrets are being told. People are making choices that will change their lives forever.

"I understand why we are all wary of Karn and Ibris. I certainly am. But we don't have enough information yet. We have all made decisions in the past that we regret."

Tarek looked across the table at Leon, who tilted his head in acknowledgment.

"Leon and I felt called to come here. We followed that call. Wren, I suspect you followed that same call.

"Karn, I don't know which call you followed because we don't know what side you are on. But, I will suspend judgment until we know more.

"Ibris. Well. If you are for real, we are happy to have you here. You—and maybe Karn—may be the key to understanding how to defeat the three men who started this whole thing.

"Now that we know that they have magical abilities, we need to know what kind of magic. How powerful is it?

"But right now, I would like to take a break. Silke and I need to speak to Ibris on our own. No, I am not going to hide what we talk about, but I have a feeling we have something to discuss first. Am I right, Ibris?"

Ibris bowed his head and said, "You are."

Tarek stood, "Okay, it's break time. Please keep from speculating about what's going on until we come back."

No one said anything as they all stood, stretched, and returned to their rooms. If they couldn't talk about what was going on, it was best to remain silent. As Meg started to go with Suzanne, Tarek reached for her hand.

"I think it would be a good idea for you to be part of this," he said.

"Why? I don't know anything about what you are talking about."

"That's one reason why. You don't know. You will be able to see things outside of the picture of what the rest of us take for granted. Besides, I think it might be a good idea for you to hear what we are going to say for personal reasons."

Meg lifted her green eyes to look at Tarek. One result of not being able to shapeshift at will was that she couldn't change her appearance anymore. It was disconcerting to her. She always matched the way she looked to the desires of the other person. She could always get what she wanted that way.

When Tarek looked at her, he saw only Meg. It amazed her that he liked the way she looked. She couldn't use her powers anymore to manipulate, and finding that people accepted her as the person she was still amazed her. Now Tarek was trusting her enough to listen to something so important he had to do it in private.

It shocked Meg to feel how her heart seemed to swell inside her chest and that she could barely hold her emotions in check. Sometimes she felt as if her body was betraying her. But at this moment, she accepted that she was being given a gift.

"Thank you, Tarek," Meg said. And then glancing at Silke sitting on Tarek's shoulder, she added, "Thank you too, Silke. I appreciate that you must want me to be here too."

Silke giggled, fluffed her hair, and then smiled.

Silke knew that there was a reason that Meg had stepped through the portal, and Suzanne had followed. Meg might have thought that she was escaping, but what she had been doing was heading towards her destiny.

The portal maker might have felt that he was banishing her, but what he had done was send help to a planet that needed it.

While the three of them spoke together, Ibris stood to the side, watching. He thought he knew what Tarek wanted to talk about. After all, what were the odds that there were two wizards on the Islands? Yes, it was time to let them know why.

Thirty-Seven

After meeting with Dax and Ibris, Stryker went back to his room. To calm himself, he opened the map again. He wanted to know if it would still show him the cave. He needed to double check before he went there to search for the next section of the pendant. Since he was alone, he reached up and felt the part of the pendant he had found, hoping some of its power would flow through him now.

But there was nothing from the pendant and nothing from the map. That meant he had to wait before committing to the search. Otherwise, he could blunder into something or someone and give himself away. He knew it wasn't worth it to rush, but sometimes the fickleness of the map made Stryker so angry he could have torn it up and thrown it into the fire, or put it out into the storm and let the storm rip it to shreds.

But not today. Today Stryker decided to trust the map and not do anything. He couldn't have gone to the cave today anyway. Although the storm was dying down, it was still too dangerous to venture out into it.

He had to admit to himself that the map didn't want him going after the pendant right now. Instead, he was supposed to do something else. The trouble was, the map never gave him any clear guidance. He always had to guess. What was he supposed to be doing?

After talking with Ibris and Dax, he had felt a little better. He wasn't alone in his worries. But that didn't mean that they were on his side.

He missed the days when he believed that there were people truly on his side. Back in the boy's school with Aaron and Sawdi, he felt as if they were a real team. But he was probably mistaken.

After all, he had never told them about the map. He had it at school with him, but he never showed it to anyone. So if he was hiding a secret, they might have been all hiding something from each other.

But still, it had been fun. However, after designing the way to take over Thamon together, things had changed. Aaron had become a total jerk. Now he was an even bigger one. What did Aaron need more wealth for?

People bowed to him three times a day for zuts sake. And Aaron's decree to take from the people of Thamon was eventually going to make the people turn against them all.

If Aaron would leave it alone, the people would voluntarily give Aaron everything he needed or wanted. No. He had to take more and ruin everything.

The coming rebellion was another reason Stryker knew that he had to find all of the pendant's pieces as quickly as possible. If he had it before the resistance happened, he could stop it on his own.

Plus, he wouldn't need, or fear, either Aaron or Sawdi. And even though he wasn't interested in gold and jewels like Aaron, he was interested in never worrying about his safety again. He would have all the power he wanted to keep himself safe and satisfy his modest physical needs.

The other reason for his increasing anxiety was the coming of Sawdi's Warrior Monks. Because he knew they would come. Sawdi had just been waiting for a reason to bring them back.

Stryker thought back to what he now thought of as simpler, happier times as they began their conversion of the people to Aaron-Lem.

Aaron sat on the throne as he had wanted to, and Stryker was happy with his armies. They had quickly taken over the first few villages that had resisted the conversion. It was glorious. Dax led the military into the villages, and Ibris followed up with his words.

Stryker sighed. What a time that had been. The boys he had trained were good at what they did. They were either army, or Kai-Via, or Preachers.

But then Sawdi revealed what he could do. Sawdi had raised the dead from those first few villages. After that, it was Sawdi's army of Warrior Monks that did most of the work, and Stryker's troops came in after it was over.

Stryker gritted his teeth at the memory. He had been humiliated. How Sawdi raised those zonking people from the dead was a mystery. One he never shared with Aaron or Stryker.

After Thamon was under the more passive control of the Kai-Via and Preachers, Sawdi retired to his cabin and stored the Warrior Monks somewhere. Relative peace reigned.

Now Aaron wanted more, which meant that Stryker had to enlist the help of Dax and Ibris to make sure Aaron got what he wanted or else Sawdi would unleash his precious army of dead people onto the Islands.

However, if he found all the pieces of the pendant first, perhaps he could stop them.

As Stryker waited out the storm and the map's refusal to help him, he thought back to his boy's training camp.

There had been a boy there then that he had started to train as a preacher. But eventually, it became clear that the boy was not suited for that, and it took some time to figure out where to place him.

Once he realized how bright Karn was, and how much he noticed, he trained him to be his eyes and ears. Sometimes the things that Karn saw and reported back to him were amazing, and Stryker used the information to control and teach the boys more effectively.

However, without warning, that boy had turned into a dragon. It had shocked them both. There was nothing he could do but throw him into a cell, while he figured out how to hide him from Aaron and Sawdi.

But one day, the door of the cell was open, and the boy was gone. At the time, he had thought that Sawdi had discovered Karn on one of his visits and had eliminated him. He had been afraid to ask. After all, keeping a dragon, even in a cell, was not allowed.

Stryker wondered what had really happened. Had he seen something he shouldn't have? What had he seen? Had Sawdi killed him? Or maybe Sawdi had saved Karn for himself, along with the other five dragons he controlled.

Of course, there was a very slight possibility that Karn had escaped and was still alive.

Stryker stroked his pendant and wondered if that were true, and if he found him, would Karn still be willing to spy for him?

Thirty-Eight

Meg watched as Ibris and Tarek once again stared at each other across the room. It seemed ridiculous to her that they stood so far apart. She and Silke exchanged looks and then smiled at each other. Men. Even wizards didn't seem to know better.

The four of them had moved to a smaller room, but neither Tarek nor Ibris seemed to know what to do next. Tarek looked over at Meg, and she realized he wanted her to run the meeting. *Why not?* Meg thought to herself. *Maybe I can be good at something.*

Pausing for a moment to get her bearings, Meg said, "I believe that you have something you want to share only with Tarek and Silke, well, and now me.

"But, first, I want to know if there is a reason why two wizards showed up on the same Island. Probably everyone else wants to know that, too. And since I don't understand how Thamon works, are wizards common here?"

"Could we sit instead of standing?" Ibris asked, gesturing to the small table in the room that they had chosen.

"Yes, there is a reason why the two of us are here, and I know you must want to know how I managed to be a wizard and a

Preacher at the same time. But if I could ask a question first?" Ibris said, looking at Meg.

"Where did you come from? Don't be offended, but you and your sister, I assume she's your sister, have a different way of speaking than I am used to."

"Fair enough," Meg said. "You're right. My sister and I aren't from this planet. I was running away from home and asked a portal maker to send me someplace beautiful, and he did.

"I should have said someplace beautiful where I could be free, but it never occurred to me that he would send me to someplace that banned magic.

"My sister, because she has always looked after me, found the portal maker and had him send her here too."

"And what are you?" Ibris asked.

Meg knew what he meant but hesitated before answering. What if he was there to betray them?

But Tarek gave her a slight nod, which she took to indicate that it was okay, so she said, "I used to be a shapeshifter who could be anything. Now, most of the time, I am Ordinary. My sister, however, is a dragon."

When Ibris looked at Meg with compassion in his eyes, it threw her off balance. That was the last thing she had expected. Kindness from a Preacher of Aaron-Lem? Could he be faking that?

"I'm sorry to hear about you losing your shapeshifting powers. It must be hard for you, but I can assure you that you are anything but Ordinary. Not to mean that Ordinary means you are less than someone with magical skills. I don't believe that at all. What I mean is that you may feel as if the portal maker banished you here, but I don't think that is true.

"There is a reason for you being here, and even though I hardly know you, I think your shapeshifting right now is going on within you, which is a very powerful thing to be happening. I think that Tarek and his Okan companion know that too."

Meg didn't have time to respond because Silke laughed, and Tarek looked taken back by her reaction.

"Where is your Okan companion, Ibris?" Silke said.

"Do you know him?" Ibris responded.

"You know I can't lie, so I can't say that I do until you tell me his name," Silke answered, her feathery hair lifting off her head as the light within her blinked on and off rapidly.

Meg wondered if it blinked at different rhythms depending on the Okan's emotions. Silke looked over at her and nodded yes.

It was Meg who asked, "So, if you are a wizard, don't you always have an Okan with you? How could you have hidden that from everyone? How can we believe you that you are a wizard, and even if you are, how do we know you are a good one? Meaning someone that does good.

"And you asked where I came from, but what about you? Where did you come from? Before Stryker's training camp, I mean."

"I can answer all those questions," Ibris said. "But first, let me ask one of Tarek."

Meg tilted her head to the side and looked at the man in front of her. There was something about him that seemed familiar, but she couldn't figure out what it was. Perhaps he reminded her of someone from Erda.

"Could you ask Leon to join us?" Ibris asked.

Silke left the room and returned with Leon, who arrived carrying a chair, knowing that there were only three chairs in the room.

Once he was settled, Ibris turned to Leon and said, "You and Tarek's mothers are sisters, correct?"

Tarek and Leon looked at each other. "Correct," Leon responded. "So what? Anyone could figure that out."

Ibris nodded and continued. "And Tarek's father, Udore, is a wizard, and he had two brothers. Did you ever meet the brother named Ian?"

Tarek stood up so quickly that his chair would have fallen over if Meg hadn't caught it.

"You said, my father is a wizard. What do you mean is? And how do you know about Ian?"

"Please," Ibris said, "Let me continue."

Meg touched Tarek's hand and gestured to his chair. "Sit down, Tarek. Let's hear what he has to say."

Leon turned to Ibris and said, "Once. I met Ian once. He and his wife stopped by because they were moving. I barely remember him, though. And later, my dad told me that the family had died when their ship went down, so I never thought about it again."

Then Leon paused and took a deep breath. "Wait. They had a son."

"Yes, they did," Ibris said. "That was me."

Thirty-Nine

"You're lying," Tarek shouted. "You are not! We are not related."

"But we are, Tarek. And to make it worse from your point of view, you are also related to Dax, the head of the Islands' Kai-Via."

Silke whispered something in Tarek's ear, and he sat back in his chair, but nothing about him had relaxed. Meg put out her hand, but he pulled back, unwilling to be touched.

Meg looked at Silke, who nodded, so Meg asked the next question. "Assuming we believe you, we need more information. Why doesn't Tarek know that he is related to you? And now you say that Dax is too. Explain."

"As I said, Tarek's father had two brothers. Each brother had a son. Tarek's father, Udore, was the oldest, and Tarek was a teenager by the time the other two brothers had children. He never met any of us because he was always off doing his wizarding thing.

"Leon met our family because, unlike Tarek, he had stayed home. I remembered you, Leon, because I wished I had a big brother like you.

"No, we didn't drown. We had settled in a village. Later that village was destroyed. It took many years before I realized that it was Stryker who had destroyed it, but saved me because he wanted me in his training camp.

"Like all the boys that he took, I don't think it was because of who we were. He was choosing young boys because he saw us as trainable.

"At the time, I didn't know that I had inherited my father's ability to be a wizard. Sadly, neither did my father. He and the Okan who served him perished in our village, which is why, Silke, I am not blessed with having an Okan like you."

Silke dropped her head, and Meg could see that she was crying.

Ibris waited for a beat before continuing.

"I'm sorry, Silke. I know that Okans are a vanishing species, and even if you didn't know my father's Okan, it is a tragedy. Like all of what is happening in Thamon."

Leon asked the next question. "So since Tarek is my cousin because our mothers were sisters, and you and Tarek are cousins related by your fathers, that means we are also related?

Ibris nodded. "It's hard to take in, I know. There are so many questions. Not only are we related, but why are so many of us from the same family here on the Islands? And then, of course, there is Dax. He's here, too."

"And also related to Tarek?" Leon asked. "I don't remember ever hearing his name when I was growing up."

Leon turned to ask Tarek if he had heard about a cousin named Dax, but Tarek's face was frozen in a cross between anger and sorrow, so Leon turned back to Ibris to hear what he had to say.

"Yes, the third brother had left when he was young and never returned. From what I can piece together, there was a falling out with the family when Dax's father realized that he was not a wizard.

"It made Dax's father mad he wasn't a wizard. For some reason, he thought it was the family's fault and didn't want anything else to do with them.

"I was not aware of Dax until we met at Stryker's training camp. We became friends, and after talking about our families together, we finally figured it out.

"Dax was angry like his father when he realized that he wasn't a wizard, either. And so once I started to realize that I was, I kept it to myself. Besides, by then, we knew that Mages, wizards, and shapeshifters, were being banished, killed, destroyed, all over Thamon.

"I decided never to tell anyone. Become the best Preacher that I could, and perhaps save people from Aaron's reach by converting them as easily and quickly as possible."

Tarek made a noise that sounded to Meg like a growl.

Ibris looked at him and said, "Yes. I know. Maybe that wasn't enough. But it was only me—first, only a young boy and a wizard with no training. And then as I got older, the danger had increased, and it was still only me. But I have done what I could without revealing myself.

"However, when I heard that Sawdi was recalling the Warrior Monks, I knew my time of non-action was over.

"Besides, Dax decided to also betray Stryker by telling me about all of you in the cave, and once I realized that there were so many of you, I knew we had a chance."

Meg listened to what Ibris was saying, nodding in understanding as he spoke, and then said, "I have questions. How much does Dax know? And just because he helped save us, does that mean he is on our side, or more that he is afraid of whoever the Warrior Monks are? And, of course, does he know that Tarek is here and that he is related to him?"

"Excellent questions, Meg. How wise Tarek is to have you here with us. I can answer these, but then I have to go before Etar rises.

"Stryker will notice that I am not there, and I need to prepare for the service."

Tarek made another growling noise at the mention of the services, and Meg turned to him and laid a hand on his leg.

"Tarek, I know this is all new to you. I know how that feels having arrived in this strange place, trusting no one. I have had to learn how to listen and decide who to trust.

"Like trusting you, Tarek. I know that you can hear that Ibris has a heart like yours. He did his best, which is more than I can say for myself when I only cared about myself.

"But I am this person now, and Ibris is here wanting help to stop Aaron-Lem. Now that he has been here, he is not safe anymore. We have to protect him, just as we do for each other."

Tarek looked at the Meg, and his face softened. "At least I was wise enough to have you lead us in the discussion."

"Yes, you were!" Meg laughed.

"Now, Ibris, we are listening, then we need to get you back to the Temple."

Ibris smiled. "Yes, Meg, you are here in Thamon for a reason. No, I don't think Dax knows exactly who is on the Islands, just that someone rescued the Mages from the destruction of the prison camp.

"No, I don't understand why he decided to save them when before he was trying to kill them, but yes, it could be because of the Warrior Monks.

"And as far as I know, Dax doesn't know that his father had another brother and he had a son. But if he doesn't know, he will figure it out.

"And lastly, although I love Dax like a brother, he is an angry man, and I am not planning to tell him what is happening, any more than I let him know that I am a wizard.

"Now, I must go. I suggest you ask Karn more questions. While he was at the training camp, he learned things he never told us. He has secrets.

"Please keep sending Samis to the services so I can communicate through him. I knew he wasn't converted the first time I saw him, and have been placing a protective shield around him so that any of the Kai-Via didn't notice, including Dax.

"And since you now know I am a wizard, I'll just take my leave the easy way."

There was a momentary disruption that was barely noticeable in the air, and then he was gone.

Leon's "Zounds!" said it all.

The four of them sat in silence for a moment, and then Meg said. "It's time to talk to Karn."

Forty

There was a quiet knock on the door, and when Leon opened it, Karn stood there." I suppose you want to talk to me next?"

Leon opened the door the whole way, and Karn came in and took the seat that just moments before was occupied by Ibris.

Meg took up the questioning again.

"Since you knew that we wanted to talk to you, perhaps you could explain your part in what is happening.

"Because even for someone like me who is just learning how to be part of other people's lives, it is apparent that the gathering of people coming to the Islands who know each other is not by chance."

Karn took a moment to look at each person in the room and then returned to Meg.

"Everyone has a gift, don't they? Although I did shapeshift into a dragon, I have one skill that I have used my whole life, even before Stryker took me."

"And what is that skill, Karn?' Meg asked.

"I am a spy."

He paused and waited for it to sink in.

As Tarek started to rise, Karn lifted his hand and said, "Let me explain. It doesn't mean that I am a traitor. It means that I know how to find things out. I am an observer. I notice things.

"I don't know exactly how it works, but I do know that I put pieces of information together that don't seem to go together, and then something clicks, and I know things others have missed.

"Once I discovered this skill, I practiced it. I tried to see and hear everything going on around me at all times. I start with assuming that people are lying. Instead of thinking that things work out for the best, I believe that they don't always. That means I see what doesn't work.

"Yes, that sometimes makes me hard to be around, and sometimes I wish I wasn't like this. I have acted out because of it. But I am wiser now, and understand that I need to accept who I am, just as everyone else does.

"What I am is a person that knows secrets. Not because people tell me. With my point of view about the world, very few people believe in me. They assume that because I know that they are probably lying, they think that I am too. The funny thing is, I am not. But when details don't mesh, I am immediately aware of them.

"When Wren and I were children, I didn't know how to use that skill. In fact, it made me mad. Why couldn't I be like everyone else and trust that what I saw and heard was true? Amazingly, Wren liked me, because even my parents were a little leery of me. They couldn't keep anything from me. I always figured it out.

"What I didn't trust was my sense that something terrible was coming before Stryker sent his armies. The signs were so obvious. Maybe that's why. They were so obvious, and everyone seemed to be ignoring them.

"I thought, being just a young boy, that I was wrong. But as you know, I wasn't.

"Instead, our village was destroyed like so many others, and my family killed. Why? Because Stryker wanted boys to train.

"That place was terrible for me. The other boys accepted, at least then, that they had been rescued by Stryker and were happy to be given something to do. Within days I knew it was all a lie. The signs were there. I don't trust, remember? That meant I looked for how I was right.

"The only thing I knew to do was learn everything that I could to help me survive. Although I mourned Wren because I thought she might be dead, I knew that if she were alive, she would come for me. If she wasn't, I would take my revenge against those that killed her once I knew their secrets.

"I knew Wren was watching long before I saw her. There were little signs. But I knew she was waiting for the right time to help me escape, so I doubled my efforts to gather every bit of information that I could. It's how I knew that Ibris was becoming a wizard probably long before he did."

Meg started to say something, and Karn raised his hand and said, "I'll answer all your questions, but it would be easier to let me tell this story.

"I have kept secrets for so long I want to tell someone something. I naturally don't trust any of you, but at the same time, I have to, because I can't stop what has happened on my own. Besides, Wren believes in you, and I will always believe in her.

"Yes, I know she doesn't trust me either, and I understand why. But I do trust her, so I am choosing to tell you all of this. I only ask that for now, no one else knows.

"Probably everyone that is here in this building is trustworthy, but they may tell someone without realizing it. Maybe someone who like me who collects information and pieces it together.'

Meg answered for all of them, "I say that yes, we will keep it a secret unless it puts someone in danger, not knowing. Agreed?"

Silke laughed. Tarek smiled. Both of them thinking that they had been right about Meg, and maybe she was learning it too. Her talent was not shapeshifting. It was more than that.

Karn nodded. "Agreed. You have heard of the Warrior Monks that are coming."

Leon broke in, "Are they coming?"

"Yes, they are," Karn replied. "The signs are there. It won't be long now.

"Sawdi, their creator, knows that Stryker is up to something, and is going to use Aaron's decree to collect from the people to send them to the Islands."

"I don't know who those Monks are," Meg said.

Karn paused before answering. Then taking a deep breath, he said, "They used to be people. Sawdi went to the villages and gathered the dead and transformed them into something more dangerous than the armies that killed them.

"These are the Warrior Monks. They took over Stryker's armies, and they are the ones that swept through Thamon killing as they went. Aaron took credit for them, but they really belong to Sawdi.

"You can hear them coming. It's like a swarm of angry bees. But you can't always see them. They are like wisps of smoke, that disperse in the air. They are unstoppable. Only Sawdi knows how to control them.

"After the conversion of Thamon to Aaron-Lem, he 'retired' them. Since then, he was off pretending to be some kind of holy person in a remote cabin in the mountains. Instead, he was planning his new invasion of the Monks."

Meg stared at Karn. "If you are telling the truth, what can

we do? Is there a way to stop them?"

"Perhaps. I think I discovered something that will work. But to make sure, I need to let Stryker find me and then go work with him. And I need to do that today."

Forty-One

"I can't stop you, can I Karn?" Wren said. They were meeting again in the small room, just the two of them.

"I wish you could, Wren," Karn replied. "I wish there were a different way, but someone has to help Stryker, and that person has to be me. He remembers me. He knows that I know things, and I can convince him that I am here to help because I heard about Aaron and Sawdi's plan."

"But what if he discovers that you are not on his side?" Wren said.

Karn gazed at his wife, thinking that after all this time, she was as beautiful as she had always been. He knew that she was able to hold the look of youth, no matter how old she was, but it wasn't what she looked like that he loved. He loved that she saw the world the way he wished that he could. She saw it as full of good people, trying to do the right thing.

And at the same time, she was clear that greed drove some people away from goodness. And others were born evil.

She knew that, and yet she could hold hope and love in her heart at all times. And still lead an army or a rescue because she had the courage of a warrior.

No, he wasn't that way. He only saw what was wrong. He

expected people to be bad, which is what had driven a wedge between them years before. He went looking for trouble.

She spent her time helping people out of it. When he realized how hard he was making life for Wren, he left. Not because he wanted to, but because he believed it was the best thing for her.

But fate had brought them back together, and this time he was wise enough to explain what he was doing and that he was always doing it for her. If he died in the process, he would die happy if it saved her, and her friends.

Wren looked into his eyes. Eyes that were always mischievous and a manner that was always smirking and saw what he meant to say, but couldn't.

"How can we help you, Karn," she finally asked, realizing that since he was going to do what he thought was right, the only thing she could do was help him.

Karn tipped his forehead down to Wren and whispered, "Pretend not to know me if you see me. Trust that if you see me doing what I am going to have to do, that it is for all the right reasons.

"You rescued me. Let me rescue you, and all these people that you care about."

For the first time in many years, Wren threw her arms around Karn and sobbed. She didn't need to tell Karn that she had never stopped loving him.

After a few minutes, Karn stepped back and said, "Let me go now. If I can, I'll be back. If not, know that I have always been, and always will be, yours."

Wren nodded and tried to smile through her tears. "I'll be waiting, Karn. Be safe."

Karn didn't smile. He nodded, turned, and walked out the door.

Wren remained, looking at the space where he had been standing just moments before, thinking of all the years that they had been apart, and she had told herself that she didn't miss him. Now that he was gone again, she admitted to herself that she had been lying to herself. There had always been an empty space, filled with loss and bitterness.

She had thought that he had left her because he didn't love her. Only now did she realize that he had stupidly assumed that she was better off without him. Maybe he was right then, but now? Now, she wanted this nightmare to be over because perhaps they had a chance to be husband and wife again.

Something had shifted within her, and she thought that now she could understand that his seeing the world differently was something she could live with, and maybe even enjoy. Sometimes.

As she admitted that Karn would always be hard to live with, Wren laughed. Yes, she would have to have more patience, but it was a price she was willing to pay to be with him again. If all went well, all of them would be free to be themselves. That was what it was all about, wasn't it?

Meg poked her head into the room, and seeing Wren standing in the middle of the tiny space with red eyes, came in and threw her arms around her. Which only made Wren cry again. Once she had sobbed on Meg's shoulder for a few minutes, she whispered, "Who are you? What happened to that wild-child?"

Meg laughed. "I have no idea. I think I am still that wild-child, but it appears to be directed towards doing something meaningful, and not just being wild and carefree."

"Well, how about something carefree right now and still meaningful. It's light out, can you shapeshift into anything? I would love to go outside and fly around for a while. Can you come with me?"

"How did you get so smart, Wren? That sounds like the perfect thing to do right now. I think I can manage a fly around. Now that our ban on doing magic has been breached anyway, why not? Let's tell Tarek what we are doing so he doesn't worry."

"Tell me what?" Tarek said, coming around the corner.

"Wren and I are going to go for a short fly around," Meg said.

Tarek smiled and said, "I don't need to tell you to be careful, do I?"

Meg stood on her tiptoes and kissed Tarek on the cheek.

"You wild-child you," Wren whispered.

A few blocks away from the deserted building, Karn glanced up to see two ravens watching him from a tree. To not give them away, he pretended not to see them. But his heart leapt, knowing that it was Wren and Meg. They were reminding him that he was not alone anymore.

For that brief moment, Karn felt at peace for the first time in many years. He had a clear purpose, and he would fulfill it or die trying.

But at least he had told Wren how he felt. That was enough for now.

Forty-Two

Karn decided that the best course of action was a direct course of action, so he crossed the Arrow and walked straight to the Temple on Hetale.

As he walked, he let the part of himself that was sarcastic, and rudely uncaring, come to the foreground. It wasn't that hard. He *was* uncaring and sarcastic. But he was more than that. And that was what was driving him now.

There were hardly any people out walking, which wasn't that surprising. It was cold, and as always, during the winter months, there wasn't much sunlight. But Karn knew that the reason people weren't out enjoying the day was more than that. They had begun to feel the effects of Aaron's dictates. Giving up the gold and jewelry was unpleasant, but the idea they would give up their livelihood would have already started them worrying.

Besides, there was the sense of betrayal they must be feeling. The people had trusted that if they followed Aaron-Lem, they would always be comfortable. They could contently live within its tenets for the rest of their lives. The discovery that things were not what they had believed would not be readily accepted. The drugged water in the chalice would not keep them happy forever.

As Karn walked up to the doors of the Temple, he transformed himself into the person that would help Stryker betray Aaron, and defeat Sawdi. In the process, he hoped that he didn't lose himself, because assisting Stryker would require him to contain the revolution.

That is unless Karn could convince Stryker to use the Mages' help to gain the control that Stryker wanted. That way, Karn wouldn't be working against his new friends. They would be working together.

One of the first things Stryker would want from him was help finding the next part of the pendant.

That would be easy. He knew where it was. It was another reason he had gone to the cave. What Stryker didn't realize was Karn knew about the map. And he knew where the next section of the pendant was in the cave. He had checked while he was hanging out with the Mages. But he left it so he could earn Stryker's trust by finding it for him.

It was his gift of noticing that had revealed the map to Karn years before as a boy in the training camp. In the same way that he had noticed Sawdi's ring and what it did.

These symbols of power meant nothing to Karn. He knew how power corrupted. It was only when he realized that the battle was shifting to the Island where he knew Wren had gone, that he had decided to step in. Up until then, he had deluded himself into thinking that he could stay out of the battle.

As he knocked on the door, Karn snickered to himself. It turns out, that wasn't what fate had planned for him. Now he was in the middle of it, and it was too late to turn back even if he wanted to.

****

Something wasn't right. Aaron couldn't put his finger on it. Even his bejeweled throne room was not bringing him any pleasure. From all over Thamon, his armies were bringing in gold and jewels.

It was piling up in every room in his Palace, and he had craftsman working on building gold statues of himself, laying gold floors everywhere, and embedding jewels in every wall available. He had always wanted to live in a jewel box, and that was precisely what he was creating.

But he didn't feel happy. He thought that Sawdi would be impressed. Instead, Sawdi had first sneered at what he had built and then ignored it all. He shouldn't have been surprised. Sawdi had never seemed to care about beauty. Sawdi had always baffled him. What did Sawdi want from what they had built together, anyway?

Even making up rituals had lost its pleasure. Aaron thought that perhaps he needed to make them more interesting. They were so passive. What would spice up the ceremonies? Aaron knew that Stryker's Preachers and Kai-Via were keeping the peace in most of the towns in spite of the new decrees he had made. Perhaps he needed to shake it up a bit.

Because of his daydreaming, Aaron hadn't noticed Sawdi enter the room and sit beside him at the table. Disturbed from his reverie, Aaron was surprised to discover that he not only didn't feel happy, he was a little afraid. Was it Sawdi that brought fear with him?

Sawdi touched Aaron's ring-covered hand and pushed into his mind, "That's not a good idea, Aaron."

For a moment, Aaron wondered if Sawdi meant it wasn't a good idea to be afraid of him, but then he realized he probably meant it wasn't a good idea that he shake things up.

Although they could speak to each other without words,

Aaron didn't like it, so he asked out loud, "Why not?"

To anyone else, Sawdi's look would have been enough to answer the question. But Aaron had grown to think of himself as a god, and gods had all power. Why couldn't he do whatever he wanted to do?

"Because you are not a god, Aaron," Sawdi answered, knowing precisely what Aaron had been thinking.

"If you push too hard, the people will rise up against you, and they will find the gods that you have forced them to abandon and use that faith to defeat you."

"What do you mean, me?" Aaron snapped. "You and Stryker are in this too."

"My point, exactly," Sawdi replied. "You are not God. We designed this religion together. But not surprisingly, we are no longer a united front."

"Meaning what?" Aaron asked, a little more fear creeping into his heart.

"Stryker plots against you," Sawdi hissed.

Aaron got up from the table and started to pace the floor, his boots scraping the soft gold as he walked. It didn't matter. A Blessed One would come in and fix the floor after they left. They would crawl in, and feel every inch of the floor for scrapes and scratches. For a moment, Aaron's thoughts flashed to a secret that he was keeping from everyone. It was his long term power play. He was sure no one knew about it, and he was going to keep it that way.

"I knew it," Aaron yelled. "I knew something was going on! What do we do?"

Sawdi smiled to himself. It was all working out as he planned. His answer was what he had planned to say years before, and now it was time.

"We stop Stryker."

Forty-Three

Someone was knocking on the door. Dax was the only one available, and he wasn't happy about being the keeper of the door. He was too important to be doing this. He had sent the rest of the Kai-Via out into the town to make sure there were no gatherings of people. He had declared that meetings other than those held at the Temple were illegal. Dax wasn't sure what he would do once the warm months arrived, and the market opened. But he had time to figure it out.

Stryker, as always, was hidden in his room, and Ibris was preparing himself for the service.

Dax mumbled to himself as he approached the door.

It was probably one of the converted getting ready to complain about not enough services. He would have to do something about that, but he wasn't sure what yet.

Although he had seen Karn, and then followed his lead to rescue the Mages, the last thing Dax thought he would ever see through the door's peephole was Karn knocking on the door of the Temple. Brazen. That was Karn. He had always been trouble.

"Holy zonk! What the ziffer are you doing here, Karn?" Dax said, opening the door a crack.

Karn pushed open the door further and walked into the

Temple. "It's cold out there," he said.

"You know what I mean, you freak!"

Karn turned to look at Dax. They had not stood face to face since they were boys. Boys that had been taken from their homes, and betrayed by Stryker. But boys who had never discussed their feelings or their motivation. Now, grown men. Both of them wondered how much they could trust each other.

"What do you want, Karn?" Dax demanded, more afraid than he thought he should be. It was just Karn. But Dax knew that it was more than that. Since Karn had come to the Islands, things had changed. The most shocking of them was his own decision to save the Mages. What was that about? They were probably out there preparing to invade the Temple or rally the people against Aaron-Lem.

Why had he helped them? With Karn. The trouble maker, spy, who always knew everything. All of Dax's thoughts circled back to the question, why had Karn come to the Islands, now? He had been missing for years.

Without meaning to, Dax blurted out the next words without waiting for Karn to reply.

"What the zonk is going on. Why is everyone coming to the Islands?"

"Ah," Karn replied. "Now that is the question to be asking. Why indeed. But to answer your first question, I am here to help Stryker."

"And what if I don't want you to?" Dax responded.

"There's where you would be wrong, Dax. You want me to. Because if I don't help Stryker, and if you don't help Stryker, then these Islands will be lost. We will all be lost. Because Sawdi and Aaron will have their way, and it will not only destroy the people of these Islands but us too."

Dax looked at Karn as if he was crazy. Why would he say

something like that out loud? Yes, he might have been thinking it himself, but he hadn't the courage to face it the way that Karn obviously had.

They were both so busy staring at each other that neither one of them saw Ibris watching them until he spoke, making both of them jump a little.

"He's right, Dax. Take him to Stryker. But you two need to be more careful. Anyone could hear you."

The three men looked at each other. Were they actually going to do this? Could they? Each one of them knew something the others didn't know, and none of them were going to tell their secrets just yet. But even then, could they work together? For Stryker?

It was Karn who broke the silence by whispering. "Before I become Stryker's lackey, I need to thank you two for helping me escape Stryker's training camp.

"I know that without your help, Wren couldn't have done it. You could have told on me, loyal members of Aaron-Lem, that you were."

Ibris dropped his eyes and said, "I should have gone with you. But perhaps this is how it is supposed to be."

"Whatever," Dax said. "It's the way it is now. Come on, Karn, let's turn you over to Stryker. Ibris, I suggest that you don't know anything about this."

Ibris nodded and silently slipped away. They were committed now. Where it would take them, Ibris didn't know. He only knew that there were too many things that he didn't know about what Aaron and Sawdi were planning. Perhaps it was time to use his wizard gifts to find out more.

Alone in his room, Ibris pulled out his crystal ball. The one he used to hide what he could do with it. He claimed that it was the crystal ball that showed the weather when it had been him that had put the weather in the ball.

But, his mother's crystal ball did have power. No, she hadn't been a wizard, like his father, but she had been a Mage. She had seen the coming of Aaron-Lem and tried to tell people, but no one listened. Or didn't listen quickly enough.

Even though he had been only a boy, Ibris felt the guilt that haunted him. What if he had listened to his mother? Could he have saved his family?

Why didn't his father and his father's Okan listen? Why would they let the village be destroyed and die trying to rescue people? They did save him but they didn't need to. Now he knew that Stryker's men would have saved him because it was him that Stryker wanted, and was willing to kill to get him.

And now he, Karn, and Dax were preparing to save Stryker. It was a bitter pill to swallow. But they were only going to help enough to rescue the Islands, and then they could deal with Stryker later.

The crystal ball lay open on the small table beside the cot that was his bed. It glowed. And then it showed him what he wanted to know.

Forty-Four

The two ravens followed Karn until he reached the Temple doors. Meg and Wren watched as Dax opened the door, and Karn pushed his way inside. Once there was nothing else to see, they returned to their building, where the rest of the core team was waiting for them.

At least that was where Meg thought they were going, but Wren kept going, and Meg followed, feeling grateful that she could, at least for now.

Her waning shapeshifter abilities were never far from her mind. The nagging voice kept asking her what she would do with herself if she were not a shapeshifter anymore.

Most of the time, she pushed those thoughts behind her. Since no one had any solution to the problem or even a hint of why it was happening, there was nothing she could do about it.

It was her own private fight, and no one could solve it for her. What helped was knowing that the people she was working with valued her for more than her shapeshifting abilities.

And when she was thinking clearly, Meg knew that a new kind of power was rising inside of her.

She couldn't yet put her finger on what that power was, but she knew it was what helped her talk to Ibris and see the essence of what he was saying and who he was. It was a strange feeling, but she liked it. Meg only hoped that it would be enough if she lost all of her shapeshifting abilities.

It took Meg a few more minutes of flying before she realized that Wren was heading towards the cabin. Probably to check on Fionn, Meg thought. But when they reached the lake, Wren veered off towards the cave and kept flying.

Tarek had turned off the magical heat and light in the cave before Stryker came looking for the Mages. But Wren must have known how to turn it back on because as they arrived at the ledge where the Mages had been living, the lights flicked on.

Wren and Meg landed and morphed back into themselves. Meg leaned over with her hands on her knees, trying to catch her breath.

"What are you doing, Wren?" Meg whispered, barely able to breathe.

Taking a deep breath, she continued, "You know I can't maintain shapeshifting in the dark. I barely made it here. I could have fallen in the water and drowned."

"You know I wouldn't have let that happen," Wren said. "I would have pulled you out!"

Meg ignored the grin on Wren's face and snapped back, "But I would have been wet and cold. What were you thinking, Wren?"

Wren's stopped smiling and said, "I'm sorry, Meg. I admit that until I was partially in the cave, I had forgotten about the dark and what it does to you. I turned the lights on as soon as I remembered. I won't forget again."

Meg's breathing had returned to normal, and seeing how crestfallen Wren was, replied, "Okay. I forget myself sometimes. But what are we doing here?

"It must be important enough to have us come now and

then have you forget about what I can't do anymore."

Wren thought back to the first time she had met Meg. Meg had been so naive and at the same time self-important because she was such an accomplished shapeshifter.

To have her own body betray her must be hard, Wren thought, but it was transforming Meg into an amazing young woman.

"Thank you, Meg," Wren said. "Yes, this is important. I didn't want to say anything, because as Ibris and Karn noted, we don't really know who to trust.

"Betrayal is the name of the game. Even we are playing it by using people we don't like to stop people we don't like more.

"Karn told me that when he was here, he found the bottom of the pendant that Stryker wants and hid it. He wanted me to come to get it. We can use it as leverage."

"We aren't actually going to give it to him, are we?" Meg asked.

"We might. It still doesn't do Stryker any good. He has to find the middle of it. All the pieces have to go together before it can help him. We will have to stop him before he finds that last piece, but for now, we need to keep him on our side, and having this part of the pendant will help."

"Okay," Meg answered, "But I am still not sure this is a good idea. Maybe it would be better to destroy it and pretend that we have it. That way, no one will ever put it back together."

"If it could be destroyed, I am sure that it would have been done before."

As the two women walked across the ledge to where Karn had told Wren he had hidden the pendant piece, Meg kept asking questions.

"I don't understand, Wren. Supposedly the pendant was made by Taweo, God of the sky, for his son. Who was his son? Is it true that when his son abused the power of the pendant, his father took it back, broke it into three pieces, and hid it?

"You know that doesn't make any sense, don't you? This is just a story someone made up. What God of the sky? What son?"

Wren stopped at the back of the cave and turned to Meg. "Just a story? Stories move the world, Meg. And does it make any less sense than anything else we believe in? Perhaps it was merely a very powerful man who called himself a god. We have a man like that right now ruling Thamon, a false god.

"True or false, yes, if enough people believe it, it becomes true. This pendant has been instilled with the belief of its power for centuries. I heard of it when I was a little girl many, many, lifetimes ago.

"So yes, I believe that the pendant gives the person wearing it the ability to control thoughts and people, which is never, ever a good thing. Even if the most benevolent person had it, it would change that person, and not for the better.

"And Stryker is far from benevolent. His thoughts are already only on what he wants for himself, and never for the good of the people, so we can't let him end up with the pendant. Ever. But we do need his help right now."

As she talked, Wren walked over to a small crack in the cave's wall. It would never have been visible if they weren't looking for it. She reached inside and pulled out a small gold object.

The two women stood looking at it, wondering how this could be so important that it could destroy a planet. As Wren held in it her hand, she thought she could feel the pendant's desire to be whole again.

That's ridiculous, she thought to herself.

But Meg saw the flash of fear in Wren's eyes and promised herself that she would not ever let that pendant be made whole again. And someday she would figure out how to destroy it.

Meg didn't believe that a god would have made such an evil thing. And if there was a real god that could help her, she hoped that god would find her and tell her what to do.

Forty-Five

Samis slipped into the service just before Ibris began speaking. The seven Kai-Via stood behind Ibris facing the crowd, a reminder that they were always watching.

Until Aaron's latest decree, the people saw the Kai-Via as protection. Now, Samis could see and feel their uneasiness.

Even in the worst weather, the service would be standing room only. Today, there were empty seats.

For the first time since Aaron-Lem arrived on the Islands, Samis felt a stirring of discontent among the people. He knew that he should be delighted about having the Preacher on their side, but instead, he found himself afraid for what was coming.

It was what he had wanted, a rebellion against Aaron and his rules. But that was before he realized what kind of destruction Aaron could send.

Looking out over the gathering of the converted, Ibris noted where Samis was sitting and the fact that for the first time in months, there were empty seats. It was all happening so much faster than he had anticipated. He thought he would have more time. But the crystal ball had shown him what was coming.

And now, seeing the empty seats, Ibris knew that his time as a Preacher of Aaron-Lem had come to an end.

Behind him, Dax stirred. Ibris hoped that Dax would be able to convince the Kai-Via to protect the Islands against what was coming. Because if he couldn't, the rest of the Kai-Via would join forces with Aaron's armies and the Warrior Monks.

There was a movement in the back of the Temple, and Ibris saw Stryker enter with Karn at his side. For a moment, Ibris faltered, and the people unconsciously flinched, sensing his distraction. It had been a long time since Stryker had come to a service, either out of trust for Ibris' abilities or disinterest in what he was doing.

All Stryker wanted was for the Islands to remain calm and peaceful while he searched for the pendant. Even though Ibris knew they were going to need to partner with Stryker, it angered Ibris that is was Stryker's plan to betray Aaron and become the ruler of Thamon that could get them all killed.

Partnering with Stryker was dangerous, but if they didn't include him in their plans, they would be fighting him as well as Aaron and Sawdi. So for now, they would protect him. But not forever.

****

Stryker thought that perhaps he was going out of his mind. What was happening? He had just been thinking about Karn, and then he appeared promising him that he would help him find the pendant. But there was a price to pay. He had to agree to protect the Islands.

"From what?" Stryker had demanded.

Karn had looked at him as if he was mad. Didn't he know? Didn't Stryker know that Aaron knew that he was planning on betraying him?

Didn't he know that Aaron would want to send his armies, but that Sawdi would send the Warrior Monks instead?

The two men had stood eye to eye as Karn asked the question. Karn was claiming to be there to help him. Was it possible?

Once Karn had been a little boy that Stryker had thought would be one of his favorite pupils. Like Ibris and Dax. When Karn had disappeared, Stryker thought that perhaps Sawdi had him killed because Karn was a collector of secrets.

Of course, he couldn't ask Sawdi what happened to Karn. No one asked Sawdi questions about what he did. Everything Sawdi did was how it was supposed to be. So Stryker never asked and was never told.

But he had been right about Karn. Karn knew things. And he told the truth. Truths that most people did not want to hear. What Karn had said was not something Stryker wanted to hear, but at the same time, he had to admit to himself that he knew it was true.

Had known it was true. Had known that Aaron must know what he was doing. But he had counted on Aaron's obsession with gold and jewels and his basic indolence to decide not to bother to stop him. Until it was too late, of course.

It was Sawdi that made the difference. It was always Sawdi. Sawdi had controlled them both, but Stryker had forgotten.

Not completely forgotten, just pushed to the back of his mind. Stryker thought that he had time enough to find the pendant, and then he would have more power than Sawdi. Than anyone, really. Then he would be safe to do whatever he wanted. Stryker didn't want riches like Aaron. He didn't even want to deal with people. He just wanted them to do what he wanted them to do. He would reinstate his training camps. He loved training those boys.

But all that was threatened because he hadn't been paying attention and now Karn was telling him what to do. Well, not telling, bribing him. Karn knew where the bottom of the pendant was.

"No," Karn had said. "It is no longer in the cave. It is safe somewhere else, and the map isn't going to show you where it is."

When Karn had said that the map didn't know where the pendant was, Stryker almost fainted. "You know about the map?" he had asked.

Karn had smirked. Stryker remembered that smirk. It had earned him attention from Sawdi. But Stryker knew that Karn smirked because he knew things others didn't know. And he knew about the map.

"Will it do any good to ask you how you know about the map? Stryker had asked.

"No," Karn had said, the smirk still on his face.

"Do other people know?"

"What do you think?" Karn had asked.

"Oh, God,' Stryker had responded.

"What god would that be?" Karn had sneered. "Certainly not the one you made up. What god do you think is going to help you?

"No. It's me who is going to help you. For now. For now, you will help protect these Islands, and then you'll get the bottom of that ziffering pendant."

"And then what?" Stryker had asked, already plotting in his head how he could overtake Karn and his friends after they stopped Aaron and Sawdi.

"Don't even think about it," Karn had said, squeezing Stryker's shoulder with surprising strength.

Stryker simpered that he wouldn't but knew Karn didn't

believe him. What was he thinking wishing that Karn would return because he knew secrets? It turned out that he did. But some of them were his.

For now, it would have to be okay, because he had hoped that somehow Karn was alive, and now here he was. He was standing beside him in a Temple watching Ibris falter.

Because he was faltering. And if Ibris was faltering, something terrible was coming.

Forty-Six

The hum was terrible. It rumbled into his bones, and it felt as if his blood was boiling in response to that sound. Aaron wanted to put his hands over his ears, but he couldn't.

He was God. He couldn't be bothered by those horrible wraiths that had been pouring into the land around his castle for the last day.

Where had they come from? He knew that Sawdi had a few Warrior Monks, but this was much more than that. There must be thousands.

It was hard to know for sure how many there were. Those white things would float in and around, sometimes looking as if they weren't even there, and other times appearing as a mass of pulsing energy.

Aaron had once seen a jellyfish, and when those things grouped together like that, that's what they reminded him of. A massive jellyfish. Their pulsing mass rose higher than the stone wall that surrounded his Palace.

Not that he could see that wall anymore. It was hidden in the fog of white wisps. No one dared to step outside.

One of his dogs had escaped into the courtyard, and Aaron had watched as the glowing white mass surrounded the dog.

Seconds later, it was gone. The dog's scream of terror and pain proved that it wasn't an easy death.

The only person the Warrior Monks listened to—if that was what they were doing—was Sawdi. It was Sawdi who had raised this terrible army from the dead.

In all the years that Aaron had known Sawdi, it had never occurred to him that it was Sawdi that was in charge of Thamon. Yes, sometimes, he would feel a frisson of fear because he would see how Sawdi didn't care about anyone or anything.

But Aaron would always calm himself, reminding himself that the three of them were partners. Only now was he beginning to see that it was possible that all of this was for Sawdi and not for anyone else.

Thinking back on their days in the boys' school, Aaron smiled. Those had been good days. They were the kings of that school. No one opposed them. Or if they did, they didn't live long. One of the three of them would have fun figuring out how to eliminate them. Sometimes they manipulated others to do it.

That was fun, too. After it was over, the boy would wake up from the trance that the three of them had put him in to find out that they had killed his friend. Sometimes in horrible ways. It was Stryker who could talk them into doing the terrible thing. That's why Stryker became the trainer for the Preachers and Kai-Via. He was the master of manipulation.

Or so Aaron had thought until recently. Maybe it had been Sawdi all along. But he couldn't go there. If he did, he would be frozen in fear.

A few months ago, Sawdi had told him that Stryker was not betraying him. But obviously, Sawdi had known that was exactly what Stryker was doing. He must have wanted those last few months to himself, back there in that cabin in the mountains. What could he possibly have been doing there?

That is the problem, Aaron thought. *I have no idea what Sawdi wants or what he does.*

At that moment, the humming was joined by a howling that was even worse than the humming. If that were possible. But it only lasted a moment.

Glancing out his beautiful stained glass windows, Aaron could see that the white mass had howled and then parted at Sawdi's arrival.

Sawdi strolled through the passage that they made for him, and then as if he knew that Aaron would be looking, he glanced up at the window and saluted at Aaron. Then holding his arm straight out, he turned in a circle. As he did, the white mass lowered itself to the ground and stayed there.

They were bowing to Sawdi, Aaron realized.

And he also realized that Sawdi was warning him. Do what he told him to do or else.

Aaron backed away from the window, shaking so hard that his robe encrusted with diamonds splattered light across the walls of this throne room.

He was so shaken that he didn't realize what he was doing when a Blessed One entered the room to bring him his morning coffee. Without thinking, he raised his arm and shot the laser beam at the Blessed One, instantly reducing him to ashes.

For a moment, Aaron was shocked that he had done such a thing without thinking. It was the "without thinking" that bothered him. He believed that he was more in control of himself than that.

But then he began to wonder if perhaps the laser was a way that he could stop Sawdi if he needed to?

A dark shadow passed over the window, and Aaron turned to look at where it had come from.

What he saw there struck more terror in his heart than he

thought possible. It took every fiber of his being to stand and not faint at what he saw.

It was a man hovering in the air, hanging there outside his window, smiling at him. A smile that never reached any other part of his face. It was Sawdi.

Without thinking, Aaron bowed. It was instinctive. But now he knew how the Warrior Monks felt. They knew that Sawdi was their master, and now Aaron knew that too. Probably had been all along.

Sawdi saluted and was gone, appearing a few seconds later at the door of the throne room.

Aaron bowed again, and this time Sawdi laughed, a cross between a hum and a howl that swept around the room and then buried itself inside of Aaron's heart.

Forty-Seven

"How long will it take for them to get here?" Meg asked.

Ibris had returned to the rebels' headquarters, appearing out of nowhere and shocking the entire gathering of rebels even though they had been told the whole story of Ibris' betrayal of Aaron-Lem.

Silke had gone back to the cabin and asked the two men staying there to join them in Woald. They would need all the help they could get, and now that Stryker knew about them anyway, there was no point in hiding.

With the arrival of Fionn and Joseph, the room was packed. Leon plus his five men. Oiseon Todd and the six men and five women from the prison camp sat in the back of the room. Meg smiled at them, but none of them returned the smile. Meg wondered if they would ever recover from what Dax and Stryker had done to them. She hoped so. They would need them.

Samis represented the three men and one woman who remained in hiding after assisting with the Mages' rescue. They would help with whatever was needed when the time came. For now, Samis wanted them to be safe, so he asked his team to stay away.

Suzanne, Ruth, and Roar sat together on chairs near the

front of the room. None of them wanted to lead. But they would do whatever needed to be done and would provide input if asked.

The three of them had grown close. Older and wiser than most of the rest of them, they had lived through more than one set of troubles. In Suzanne, Ruth and Roar had found another kindred spirit. Another person who lived to serve, and almost always did that serving in the background.

Meg often teased Suzanne that it was a good thing she had run away because Suzanne would have never met these new friends. Although Suzanne would smile and agree with her, both of them knew that Suzanne missed her friends in both the Earth and Erda dimensions.

It was different for Meg. She never had friends before. These people had become her whole world, which still shocked her. And that she was sitting with the group of people the others considered leaders of the group was almost inconceivable.

Meg was reasonably sure that her parents had never considered this possibility for her either. For a moment the sorrow of what she had done passed over her, but she shook it off. It wouldn't help her here.

A small table had been set up at the front of the room, and that was where she, Tarek, and Wren were sitting, facing the group. Tarek was beside her with Silke on his shoulder. Wren was on the other side. The larger table they had been sitting around had been replaced with chairs found throughout the building.

It was Wren who had explained to the group what Karn was doing. She told them that for now, Ibris, Dax, and even Stryker were on their side. The news had not gone over well with the Mages.

A huge shout of "no" sounded from the back of the room,

and all the men except Oiseon stood up and walked out. It was the first that they had heard about what was going on.

The women remained but wept quietly in their chairs.

Meg realized that it had probably been a mistake to keep the Mages protected and out of the loop. Now they were trying to catch up with the idea that the people who had tortured and killed their friends and family would now protect them.

The women kept shaking their heads at the news. There was no way that the most important Preacher in Aaron-Lem was on their side. Let alone that he was a wizard. And as far as Dax and Stryker were concerned, there was no possibility that they were on their side.

Tarek took over from Wren and explained that they might not always be on their side. But the Warrior Monks had been triggered because Aaron had heard that Stryker was betraying him. Stryker knew that he couldn't fight the Monks on his own, and that was why he was willing to partner with the people he had hated.

Tarek left out the part about a third man controlling both Aaron and the Warrior Monks. Learning about Sawdi would have to come later. First, they needed everyone in the room to be on the same side.

The six men who had walked out had returned to the room and were standing in the back listening, trying to make up their minds if what they heard was real, or if their leaders were betraying them, or stupid.

Oiseon gestured to them to sit and listen, and they reluctantly joined him and the women. Meg smiled at them again, hoping something had changed. It hadn't.

Leon was not having that problem with his men. They knew Tarek. They had trusted him before, and they would do so again.

If he said this was what was happening, then they better get ready to do what he asked of them.

During a moment of quiet, Oiseon spoke up. "Perhaps you best describe the Warrior Monks because that may explain why our enemies are willing to partner with us to stop them."

Tarek's explanation of what they were facing changed everything.

The room had become deadly silent when Meg had asked how long it would take for them to get there, and then Ibris appeared in the room.

Samis was the only one not surprised at Ibris' appearing. Ibris had slipped him a note after the service, but he had not had time to let the rest of them know before Ibris appeared.

Most of the people in the room didn't know who Ibris was until he spoke. Yes, it was true, their Preacher had magical abilities. That was shocking enough, but his words sent fear throughout the room.

"They have left Aaron's Palace and will arrive by tomorrow night. We won't see them at first. We will hear them. What we will see is their destruction.

"To stop Stryker, they will destroy everything on the Islands just because they can."

Everyone in the room stood. Meg, Tarek, and Wren remained seated. They knew what was coming next.

Forty-Eight

Leon walked out of the room and returned with three men—Karn, Stryker, and Dax. The room erupted. Tarek stood and said, "Quiet."

It was not so much his words that caused the noise to stop but a quiet field that descended over them. Meg knew it came from two directions. Ibris and Tarek had subdued the room together.

They were also doing something to Stryker because he stood as still as a stone. Or maybe he had just realized that Ibris was not only a preacher. Or perhaps it was the shock that what he was doing was the direct opposite of what he would ever consider doing before.

Ibris walked over to Stryker and whispered something in his ear. Stryker turned white. Meg heard Stryker ask, "Have you always been a wizard?"

She also heard Ibris' answer. "Yes. And you have always hidden your own desires to rule."

Dax turned to look at both Stryker and Ibris. Even though he had asked Ibris to help save the Mages, he had not entirely accepted that Ibris was a wizard, like his father. Probably because if he had admitted that he suspected it, he would have been required to stop Ibris the same way he had overcome the other Mages.

Ibris put his hand on Dax's shoulder, and the two men stared at each other. A series of pictures flashed through Dax's mind. Ibris showed him how his anger had put him on the wrong side. As he watched the images Ibris showed him, his anger began to melt away, and was replaced with a deep despair over what he had done. Was it possible to redeem himself?

As Ibris opened Dax's memory to the God that his family had served, Dax knew he might not survive the coming battle with the Warrior Monks. But perhaps if he helped save the people he had betrayed, his God would look kindly on him.

Ibris pulled Dax into a hug, and if they hadn't been standing in front of a room full of rebels, most of whom hated him, Dax would have wept.

Instead, he turned to the room and made himself say, "I am sorry."

Beside him, Stryker grew rigid. Dax was apologizing? *Karn was right. They were all betraying him. How had this happened?*

Although most of the people in the room didn't know before that Dax was the head of the Kai-Via, and the person who had held them prisoners, once they saw him with Stryker and Ibris they knew. He had been responsible for what had happened to them.

"I am not looking for forgiveness," Dax said, as Stryker grew more rigid.

"I am here to help. It will never make up for what I have done. But I was wrong. Let me help you."

The Mages at the back of the room remained frozen in various stages of shock and anger. But once again, Oiseon led the way. With one glance at his long-time friend Wren, he knew what he had to do.

He stood and walked over to Ibris and shook his hand. "Thank you," he said.

Oiseon turned to Dax but did not shake his hand. Instead, he stood in front of him and said, "We appreciate your help. May your God forgive you for what you have done. Perhaps you can put some of it right."

Finally, Oiseon turned to Stryker. "I don't trust you at all. Never will. But we will accept your help with the understanding that if we survive this, we will come after you."

Stryker wasn't worried. He was smarter than them, Besides, it wouldn't be long before he had all of the pendant, and then he would have all the power.

Karn watched all of this from the side of the room. He wanted to go to Wren, but she had stilled him with just one glance.

As much as Karn didn't want to, he understood. Until this was over, he was to serve Stryker. Not be with her.

But before Wren turned away, she patted the pocket of her tunic. Once again, Karn understood. She had part of the pendant. It was the bribe they would use to keep Stryker on their side.

****

Ibris stood inches from the face of his former teacher and leader and said, "Yes, we will need your help, Stryker, but in the meantime, we are placing you in protective custody."

Tarek gestured to Leon and Samis to take Stryker out of the room. Even though Dax had said he was on their side, Samis couldn't look at Dax. As he passed him, he whispered, "I remember what you did to my friends. I will be watching you."

Dax lowered his head and nodded. He remembered what he

had done too. He would never forget. It was as if a cloud had lifted off of him. Now, instead of anger, he felt pain. Pain so intense, he wondered how he would survive it.

When he felt someone in front of him, Dax glanced up and reeled back in shock. Facing him was the shapeshifter he had tortured and then sent to his death. It couldn't be, but it was, and that meant his time on Thamon was over. Whatever this man did to him now, he deserved it and more.

Roar reached out, and Dax instinctively stepped back. "Stop!" Roar said, and Dax moved back to face the man he had tortured.

"Please, you have a right to kill me, but let me help first," Dax said. "I have no magical skills, but I am a fighter. I can help plan how to save the Islands. Then you can kill me as I deserve."

Roar put his hand on Dax's heart. "You will suffer enough, Dax," Roar said.

"I can't stop what is going to happen to you, but I know that your mind was clouded, and is now clear. For that, I am grateful. And I forgive you. You didn't know what you were doing."

This time, Dax couldn't stop himself. He dropped his head and wept.

Forty-Nine

"Do we have time?" Meg asked the group that remained in the room.

"We have to," was Tarek's answer.

The Mages had gone off with Oiseon to discuss what they had heard and what they could do. They needed an inventory of magical skills available for them to use to save the Islands.

Meg thought that it was something they should have done before, but better late than never.

Leon and his men were guarding Stryker, which would have terrified almost everyone else. But Leon knew all of Stryker's fears. After all, he and his men had served Stryker on the ship that brought him to the Islands.

While walking to the room where they would be keeping him prisoner, Stryker really looked at Leon for the first time and then at the men that walked with him, and asked, "Do I know you from somewhere?"

Leon and his men laughed and said, "We won't be serving, or tasting, your food ever again."

If Stryker's hands had not been bound behind his back, he might have lunged at them, but he contained himself and pretended that what they said didn't bother him. Besides, he knew that he would need these people to save him from what was coming.

Privately, Leon wondered why they bothered to save this sorry excuse for a man anyway. But, he had decided that Tarek must know what he was doing. If Tarek said that they needed him then they did.

Besides, just killing Stryker wouldn't give anyone any satisfaction. This man was one of the architects of the destruction that had taken over Thamon. Death would be too easy for someone like him.

Tarek had prepared the room for Stryker. It looked like any other room, except it blocked all signals both in and out. The only communication he would be having, for now, would be with the people he had tried to eliminate and the students he thought he had trained to serve him.

The room was pleasant enough for a deserted building, but Stryker couldn't settle down. He paced the floor, fingering the top part of the pendant. There was no reason anymore to hide it, or his quest to find it. Everyone knew about it, and the map that he kept with him at all times.

When Ibris told him that he and Karn had known about it for years, Stryker had pretended not to be bothered by the revelation, but it had shaken him to his core. Part of him wanted to be pleased that he had trained his students, Ibris, Dax, and Karn so well that they were smarter than him, but that was not at all how he felt.

Although the agreement he had reached with them involved them saving the Islands, he had no intention of giving up control over the rest of Thamon, and the predicament that he found himself in at the moment only made him more determined.

Being subject to this humiliation would never happen again

once he had all three pieces of the pendant.

Karn had promised him that he would get the piece from the cave when Stryker kept his agreement to help. What exactly he was going to do to help was not clear to him. Besides, he didn't trust any of them. They had betrayed him.

He laughed at that thought. Perhaps they had learned the skill of betrayal from him. After all, he was betraying Aaron and Sawdi.

Yes, betrayal was the name of the game. Whoever was best at it would win. Trust no one. Look out for yourself only. Eliminate your competition.

That had been the tenets he, Aaron, and Sawdi had set up together. With that kind of basis, they all knew that sooner or later, only one of them would rise to the top. He had to make sure that it was him. Then he could come back for revenge.

The map, Stryker thought. Perhaps the map would show him where the pendant piece was now. Sitting at the table provided for him, Stryker pulled the map out of his pocket and unfolded it. There was only one thing on the map. A pulsing dot. Inside a building at the edge of Woald.

Stryker started to laugh. The pendant was in the building. All he had to do was find it and escape before the Warrior Monks arrived. All of this was working in his favor, after all. It proved to Stryker that he was the one who was supposed to rule Thamon.

All he had to do was get out of the room, find the pendant, and escape before they discovered what had happened.

Something tapped on the window. He looked up to see Falcon. He hadn't even called him. Once again, proof that he was on the right track. At least one of his students still obeyed him.

To open the window, Stryker had to stand on a chair. The

window didn't open wide enough to escape, but it did allow Falcon to come into the room. Falcon hopped up to the table and looked at the map. Cocking his head, he flew out of the room.

Stryker watched him go and hoped that he had gotten the message. The fact that it was Sawdi who had given him the gift of Falcon didn't bother him. It also didn't bother him that one of the boys in the camp had gone missing at the same time that Sawdi had given him the bird.

Many boys went missing at the camp. It wasn't up to him to figure out where they all went. But Falcon had spied for him ever since. If it had once been one of the boys, so be it. He called it Falcon, and it did what he asked of it.

Between the two of them, they would find the pendant and leave the Island. Let the rest of them work out how to save themselves. If it turned out that the last part of the pendant was on the Islands, he would return to get it after Sawdi had cleared the Islands of everyone else.

Yes, his former students were clever, but not clever enough.

Fifty

The noise was terrible. Aaron couldn't wait until they left. For the past day, they had been swarming in and around the Palace. Sometimes he would walk into a room, and a white wraith would be hanging in the air staring at him through the holes in what Aaron supposed was its head.

Those holes must be their eyes, Aaron thought. But to him they looked like holes that extended out behind the white thing and into nothing. The Warrior Monk would hang in the air humming, vibrating, and floating with the air currents. Its black eye holes never blinking.

Usually, Aaron would turn and walk out of the room, but that didn't save him from the wraiths. He would encounter it in the halls and even in his private chambers. Only the Blessed Ones didn't seem to be bothered by them. But then they couldn't see them, only hear the humming, and when Sawdi arrived, the howling.

The people in the villages around the Palace had been smart. They had left the area the minute they heard the humming. Aaron knew that the people remembered that noise from before when the Warrior Monks had swept through their towns, destroying everything in their path.

For the first time in his adult life, Aaron wished he was a villager and could get away from these horrible things that Sawdi had made.

But Sawdi had assured him that they were leaving today. He would be going with them, riding his favorite dragon Bolong. Aaron shivered, even though it wasn't cold. He knew who Bolong had been. He was one of the boys that Stryker had been training in his camp.

Sawdi loved visiting Stryker's training camp. It was his favorite hunting ground. During one of his visits, Sawdi had decided that he needed dragons to ride on and to use as weapons. When he returned from that visit, he had five dragons with him. And like the Warrior Monks, they obeyed only Sawdi.

Aaron hoped that Sawdi would take the whole crown of dragons with him to the Islands. *That would be a relief,* Aaron thought. He had never liked the dragons. He admitted to himself that he was afraid of them. Who wouldn't be? They were huge, and they breathed fire.

He worried that they would turn on him someday when Sawdi wasn't around to stop them. He knew the dragons would never betray Sawdi, but he wasn't included in that favored status.

Walking away from the windows where the Warrior Monks gathered, Aaron turned and sat on his throne. He rang a bell, and a Blessed One shuffled into the room, bowed at his feet, and waited for instructions. Aaron smiled. At least he had his Blessed Ones. When Sawdi was gone, he could go back to his days filled with gold, jewels, quiet servants, and his daily trips to his women.

A huge howl sounded from outside, and Aaron rushed back to the window. Yes, Sawdi was riding the largest of the dragons with the other four trailing behind. They swooped over the

Palace and the wraiths rose with them. Within seconds they were gone. Aaron breathed a sigh of relief. He was free—time to have some fun.

But when he turned to go back to his throne, he saw the wraith floating in the corner, his black eye holes burning into Aaron.

Aaron took a deep breath and returned to his throne. Okay. So Sawdi didn't trust him. So what. Perhaps this would give him a chance to figure out how to stop the Warrior Monks. What controlled them? Could Sawdi control them from a distance? Or was this one on his own?

It was time to act like the God that he was. All-powerful. Not afraid of white things, or Sawdi, or dragons.

While Sawdi was busy taking care of Stryker, he would get busy figuring out how to take his power back. He was God. Not them. Perhaps Sawdi and Stryker would destroy each other, and he would be free. But just in case that didn't happen, he needed to find out what Sawdi had told this Warrior Monk to do.

The Blessed One was still kneeling waiting for instructions. Aaron raised his wrist. He didn't know this one, so it wouldn't be much of a loss. The laser immediate destroyed the man in front of him.

The Warrior Monk didn't move.

Okay, Aaron thought. *He isn't stopping me from killing others.* But how could he find out if his laser worked on a wraith without making it mad?

He called in another Blessed One and then directed him to the corner where the Warrior Monk hung in the air. The Blessed One couldn't see the wraith, but they had long ago learned the directions of the room, so he had no problem walking to the corner to wait for instructions.

The Monk didn't look at the Blessed One. He kept his eyes

on Aaron as Aaron raised his wrist. The wraith didn't move.

Aaron fired, the Blessed One disintegrated. The wraith hadn't moved and showed no sign of having being affected by the laser.

Well, that didn't work, Aaron thought as he called in a third Blessed One and had him remove the ashes. Then he asked for breakfast. Suddenly he was hungry. Sawdi was gone, and while he was gone, he was back in power. Wraith or no wraith.

Aaron didn't know how long it would take before Sawdi returned from the Islands. He would have to make use of every moment and have a plan in place to stop Sawdi before he returned. Maybe before Sawdi even got back to the Palace. And if it was Stryker who survived, he had to be ready for him too.

How could he have forgotten that he was the God of Thamon?

Sawdi had confused him, but now he was clear. Breakfast, a visit to the women, and then a visit to his hidden treasure. Not jewels and gold this time, but a person. Someone who might be able to help him.

He would at least try, Aaron knew, if only to save his son.

Fifty-One

"Are you going to share your plan with me, Tarek?' Meg asked. The two of them were sitting together in the corner of the meeting room. Everyone had dispersed after Leon took Stryker to his room. Wren had told everyone to get something to eat and come back in an hour.

"What makes you think I have one?" Tarek answered.

Meg leaned back in her chair and studied Tarek. So many things had taken place in the last day, secrets told, revelations, and betrayals. How did Tarek feel about knowing that he was related to Ibris? The Preacher. And then to find out that he was a cousin of Dax's, the head of the Kai-Via, the person they had battled to save the Mages from just a few short months ago.

Did Tarek wonder how he, or they, could trust Dax? She had seen Dax's breakdown and apology. If anyone believed him, it should be her. She had experienced a transformation, so she knew it was possible. She was nothing like the woman who had come through the portal. If she could transform, perhaps Dax could too.

Tarek watched Meg, waiting for her next question, even though he hadn't answered her first one yet.

Meg took a drink of water before saying, "It must be odd

to find so many pieces of your family here on the Islands. Dax, Leon, and Ibris. All related to you.

You are bound together in the desire to stop the Warrior Monks from destroying the Islands. But will that bond hold? Do you trust them? And I haven't forgotten that you haven't answered about your plan."

Tarek was saved from answering any of Meg's questions by Silke. She had gone to check on Oiseon and the Mages, and her return brought her straight to Tarek's shoulder. Meg squinted at Silke, who squinted in return. That timing was a little too perfect not to be planned. So Tarek wasn't going to answer her question. If necessary, she would have to figure it out on her own.

Ibris strode into the room, followed by Karn and Dax. Wren and Suzanne were the next to enter, and then the room quickly filled with everyone else.

The Mages came in last, and once again took up their place in the back of the room. It bothered Meg that they still isolated themselves like that, but she tried to understand how they felt and not judge. Maybe it wasn't isolation. Perhaps it was about community. They understood each other. Only Oiseon remained standing, waiting for everyone to settle.

Meg, Silke, Tarek, and Wren took their place at the front of the room, and then Tarek gestured to Ibris to join them. For a moment, Ibris hesitated. *Did he belong there?* But then he realized the wisdom of sitting with the other four. It was a united front. They were showing the group that they trusted him, and it was trust that the group needed if they had any hope of succeeding.

If the Mages didn't believe him, they wouldn't help. That non-action might mean their death, but they wouldn't want to be seen as turning against all of their people alive or dead.

It would be a stupid decision, and it would guarantee the death of everyone on the Island. However, Ibris could see the Mages making that choice, thinking it was the right thing to do. Yes, they needed to trust him, and Dax, and Karn.

Dax watched as Ibris sat at the front table, and felt a jolt of recognition. *Had this happened before or had he dreamed it?* What happened next, he didn't know, but this felt as if it was supposed to be this way. But did that mean that they would all die together or live together? Stryker's presence, even locked away, terrified him.

He knew Stryker's temper. He knew what Stryker would do to them if he could. Although Stryker seemed to possess very few magical skills, he had a cunning mind. If Stryker could betray them, he would. And then he would destroy them all if he had a chance. The only thing that might save them was the fact that they controlled part of the pendant that he wanted.

After everyone was seated, Oiseon remained standing, waiting for the room to calm down. Finally, when everyone had stopped talking with each other, Oiseon spoke.

"My friends and I have discussed what we could do to help protect these Islands."

Oiseon turned to look at the Mages sitting in the back of the room and said, "We have known each other for many years, but I was not aware of many of the magical skills my friends have available for this fight.

"We have never had to be Mages to survive before. It was just something we are. Not something to flaunt. Magical skills are not that much different from any skill, whether we call them ordinary or magical.

"I am saying all this because we are rusty at what we can do, which might make a difference. Not only lack of use during our lifetimes, but the time in the prison camp drained us, and until we try, we won't know how much damage it did."

Tarek and Ibris looked at each other, and it was Tarek who spoke. "We appreciate anything that you can do. And I think that Ibris and I can increase your skills as needed.

"I wouldn't be sitting here if I didn't believe that we can do this. All of us have come together at this moment for a reason. We are here to stop the Warrior Monks, and the man coming with them, from destroying the Islands."

Turning to Suzanne, Tarek added, "And that man will be riding dragons."

Everyone turned to look at Suzanne, who had turned white. "Dragons, how many dragons?" she whispered.

It was Dax who answered. "Five. Five of them. All of them under the control of Sawdi."

Meg spoke up, "Well. Now I think we all really need to know if you have a plan, Tarek."

Tarek smiled, looked at Wren and then Karn, and said, "We do."

Fifty-Two

That morning they flew under a sky so dark it could have been night. But Bolong knew that the dark sky was an illusion. They were traveling outside of time. How Sawdi did it, Bolong didn't know, but he had experienced it before when Sawdi had first transformed him and his friends into dragons and then brought them from Stryker's training camp to their current home, a large cave near Aaron's Palace.

Although he hated being only a dragon, Bolong did appreciate the joy of flight. Even with Sawdi on his back, it was glorious to swoop and glide through the air. He could feel his friends enjoying the chance to fly too. It was easier for them. They didn't have to deal with Sawdi.

That is if they could forget about the Warrior Monks traveling with them.

If you could call what they were doing traveling. They had no sense of anything moving around them. The white wraiths that surrounded him didn't move separately. They didn't seem to be moving at all. Instead, they surrounded them as a mass, a white cloud with hundreds of empty black holes in it. The Monks showed no emotion. No life. Just directed purpose.

Bolong not only hated the Warrior Monks, but he was

also terrified of them. He couldn't read them. There was no way to figure out what they were thinking. Bolong thought that perhaps that was because they didn't think. They just did what they were programmed to do—directed to do. And that program always involved some form of destruction. Destruction that they carried out efficiently and without any apparent losses on their part.

The question that had haunted Bolong since the moment he had first learned about the Warrior Monks and what they did was, since they aren't alive, how do you kill them? Could they die a second time or even a third time?

No one knew the answers to any of the questions about the Warrior Monks. Since only Sawdi could control them, maybe only Sawdi could kill them.

Sawdi's control of the wraiths was the only reason Bolong didn't simply buck Sawdi off his back. He wanted to. He thought about it all the time. He could imagine how he and his friends would throw fire at Sawdi as he fell to the ground thousands of feet below.

If necessary, or maybe because it would feel good to them, they would tear him apart with their claws enjoying his screams of terror. Yes, Sawdi had magic to use, but perhaps the shock and terror of five angry dragons attacking him could stop him from using it.

Huddled in the cave, waiting for orders from Sawdi, the five dragons would run through this kind of scenario over and over. They weren't afraid of dying.

Banished to a life of serving Sawdi, and living as dragons with no hope of becoming the boys they used to be ever again, they had all agreed that it was worth the sacrifice of one or two, or even all of them, dying in the process of killing Sawdi.

What stopped them each time was the knowledge that the

Warrior Monks would then run free. Those horrible white wraiths would be able to do whatever they wanted to without anyone controlling them. Or they would continue to live out the programing that Sawdi had put into them. It would be the end of everyone on Thamon.

So they put their plans away each time. Sawdi couldn't die until they figured out how to stop the Warrior Monks. Perhaps that would also involve stopping Sawdi. Maybe even force Sawdi to take the spell off of them so that they could live a regular life again, although they would no longer be boys. They would be men. Bolong sighed. This was all a pipe dream.

However, once again, Bolong's thoughts turned to the boy he had once known back in Stryker's training camp. It was possible that Karn knew the secret. But most likely, he had died years ago. And even if Karn were still alive, how would he find him? And even if he could find him, did Karn really know the secret, and if he did, did he remember it?

Since there was nothing else that he could do, Bolong decided to enjoy the flight. He wasn't afraid of what could happen to him and his friends on the Islands. Between Sawdi's magic, the Warrior Monks, and dragon fire, the people on the Islands didn't have a chance.

However, one thing the dragons had decided on together is that although they would do what was expected of them to terrorize the people so that Sawdi would be pleased with them, they would not knowingly actually harm anyone.

They had to hope that Sawdi didn't notice. They were counting on him being too busy harnessing the Warrior Monks and looking for Stryker—the main goal of the mission—to see what they were not doing.

When Sawdi kicked him, Bolong recognized it as a signal that they were almost there. Time to enjoy flying before it was too late. Bolong roared with pleasure, opened his wings with the red streak running through them, and soared through time.

Sawdi loved it when Bolong flew. The strength and power of the dragon would flow through him, and for long moments he would forget everything but the joy of flying on the back of a dragon. More pleasure awaited him at the Islands, but it would feel different. This pleasure was pure.

Sawdi glanced at the ring on his finger. Its stone had grown darker. It was gathering power.

Soon, he promised it. And then he lay down on Bolong's neck and let the wind rush over him, blowing away all his thoughts. He would collect them again when they got there.

For now, it was just him and flight.

Fifty-Three

Stryker couldn't believe how stupid these people were. They had left his door unguarded. Sure, they were off preparing what to do since Sawdi was on the way, but they could have left someone to guard him. They probably thought that Tarek's power to lock him in was all they needed.

His Falcon had come and gone. He was off looking for the pendant hidden in the building somewhere. However, he could escape, he could find it himself.

Obviously, the map wanted him to get it. It kept showing him a pulsing dot that moved throughout the building. Someone had it. All he had to do was follow the dot, surprise the person, and then use Falcon to help him escape.

There was only one way off the Island. By ship. And luckily, a ship had arrived in Lopel the day before. Stryker knew that it was still docked but was scheduled to leave later today. If he got there before it sailed, he would be able to command the Soleis and have it take him to where he wanted to go. That would be wherever the map directed him.

Yes, he had agreed to help stop Sawdi, but that was before they locked him in this room. Besides, Stryker was sure they didn't know what Sawdi could do with his Warrior Monks. He had seen them from a distance, and it had terrified him. And that had been when they were on the same side. Now they would be coming after him. There was no way he was going to wait for that.

He had to get out of the room.

Falcon appeared at his window, cocked his head and projected his thoughts into Stryker's head. Of course, Falcon wasn't an ordinary falcon. He was once a boy. Since many years had passed, he would now be a man if he hadn't been permanently changed into a falcon by Sawdi and given to Stryker as a gift. Stryker saw the irony in this. Falcon would help him escape the man who locked him inside this spell.

"What did you find out?" Stryker asked Falcon.

"The Soleis is still there but is preparing to leave within the hour. They believe that a storm is coming, and they want to be far from the Islands before it strikes."

"What about the pendant, fool!" Stryker yelled, forgetting for the moment that someone could be listening. He froze, waiting for a sound. Nothing.

Turning to Falcon, who rested on the ledge of the window waiting for Stryker to hear what he had to say, Stryker gestured to him to hurry up and answer.

Pausing for a moment, the Falcon pushed to him, "The woman, Wren, has it in her pocket. But she is a shapeshifter. Not easily fooled. You know her. She and her friend were the ravens at the camp."

Stryker's face turned red. That ziffering woman. He should have gotten rid of her before. But she was only a woman, and he could overpower her since he would have the element of surprise.

It was a good thing that Karn had picked up the pendant from the cave the way he had said he would as part of their agreement. And then he gave it to a woman? Even better.

Once this was over, perhaps Karn would like to come work with him for real. He knew that Karn always figured that someone was betraying him, which made him extremely cautious. But that was a quality he could use, especially now that he would be on the run, and on his own.

Which meant he better keep the promise he had made to Karn in return for the pendant.

He had promised Karn that he would not hurt his friends. It was an easy promise to make. Even though he never kept his promises if he didn't need to, this was an easy one to keep because he had no time to stop and hurt the people on the Islands. No time, and no need. Sawdi and his ziffering Warrior Monks would do that for him.

Taking a scrap of paper from his pocket, Stryker scribbled a note to the captain of Soleis. It demanded that he wait for him no matter what. He would be paid handsomely for waiting, and cruelly punished if he didn't.

Folding up the paper, Stryker gave it to Falcon with the instructions to make sure it was understood. Peck out the eyes of anyone not willing to obey his orders.

Once Falcon was gone, Stryker turned his attention to the room. Tarek had made a mistake by leaving the window open to the outside. Perhaps he had done it as a kindness, but kindness was a weakness.

If Tarek was weak in this way, maybe his spell was not as potent as he thought. As if in answer to his prayers—if he had someone to pray to—the door of the room opened, and one of Leon's men came in with a tray of food.

"Thank you," Stryker said, smiling at the man. "Your name is Joseph, right?"

"Aye," Joseph answered, setting the food on the table.

"No one needs to taste your food today, Stryker. You were safe on the ship, and you are safe here."

Stepping up as if to see what Joseph had brought, Stryker put his hand on Joseph's shoulder and sent a jolt of energy through his hand into Joseph's neck. As Joseph collapsed to the floor, Stryker whispered, "Aye, but you were never safe on the ship, and you were not safe here."

Leaving Joseph on the floor, and the food on the table, Stryker slipped through the open door and pulled it behind him. He heard the lock click and smiled to himself.

Yes, the gods were always on his side. Now to find that woman, dispose of her if he had time so she wouldn't trouble him again, and get to the ship before anyone figured out what was happening.

They were so busy preparing for the coming disaster that they had forgotten about the disaster already in their midst. They had forgotten about him.

Fifty-Four

Standing in the small closet where she and Karn had talked just hours before, Wren took the pendant bottom out of her pocket and stared at it.

It was nothing spectacular to look at, only a small gold rectangle with a rounded bottom. It did feel good, though. She rubbed her fingers around the curve at the bottom and admired the artistry. As simple as it was, it had a beauty all its own, and to touch it was soothing.

How could this simple piece of jewelry be so important? Why would someone give so much power to an object? There would always be someone who would want to use it for evil. And if this pendant could amplify whatever power the holder already had, then Stryker having it would expand his ability to manipulate anyone to do what he wanted them to do.

That had always been her fear, but Tarek and Ibris had explained to her that it wasn't Stryker who was the ultimate danger, it was Sawdi.

Sawdi felt nothing for anyone, and no one could understand his motives or reasons for what he did. Only Stryker had the answers, and they were hidden in his heart—if he had a heart.

The pendant sat on the palm of Wren's hand, looking

innocent. Part of her didn't want to let it go, and that scared her.

Although there was nothing tangible to mark the power of the pendant, the fact that she didn't want to follow Tarek's orders, and instead wanted to keep it, meant that as innocent as it looked, it was already pulling at her. And it was just one piece. What would it be like if it was all together?

No wonder Stryker was always fingering the piece around his neck. No wonder he wanted the whole thing so much. It was a delicious feeling.

It was only out of love for her friends, and the fact that Wren always put others' safety above her wants and needs, that she was able to follow Karn's directions.

She bent down and pulled up a loose floorboard, wrapped the pendant in a piece of cloth that Karn had given her, and laid it under the board. Then she pulled the table on top of it. They had promised Stryker this piece of the pendant, and once he had saved them from Sawdi and his Warrior Monks, he would get it.

In the meantime, it wasn't safe for her to be carrying it around. Besides, they not only had to prepare for Sawdi's arrival, but there was a storm on the way too. It would be nice if they canceled each other out, but that was wishful thinking, and she had no time for that.

Wren looked back into the room before shutting the door. No one would ever know that piece was in there. It was safe for now.

****

Sawdi kicked at Bolong. A storm was racing them to the Islands. He had to get there first. They would take over the Temple and wait out the storm.

The Kai-Via would be waiting for him, even though he

was sure that Dax and Ibris would have sided with Stryker in an attempt to save the Islands. He had long ago foreseen their possible betrayal.

But the six remaining Kai-Via would be his. He had prepared for this event years before and chosen the six that served under Dax carefully. They would obey Dax as long as he remained faithful to Aaron-Lem and Aaron, which was being loyal to Sawdi. But only a few people knew that.

More would know soon who was the real power, but for now, it was better this way. To be the power behind the scenes was much better than being visible.

The six would not follow Dax in betrayal, not out of loyalty, but out of fear. Sawdi had told them that their families were safe as long as they served him. No, they would not betray him. Of course, if they knew that he had lied, that might change things. He didn't have the energy or time to deal with prisoners. The families were long gone.

Bolong dipped lower, and the rest of the crown followed. They were almost there. Sawdi loved being surrounded by the Warrior Monks. To him, they were a comfort. But to others, they were terrifying.

That pleased Sawdi. As he punched up the power he released to the Warrior Monks, Sawdi reminded himself that destroying the Islands was secondary. The first goal was to stop Stryker. For good.

****

The room was still. No one spoke. They were all in the big room together. Waiting.

Meg shook in both excitement and fear. Beside her, Suzanne squeezed her hand, acknowledging that she knew that Meg's shapeshifter powers were gone. The approaching storm had thrown the Islands into total darkness. One of the Mages used his ability to keep a few lights burning in the room, but the rest of the building was dark.

The door opened, and Joseph entered, and all eyes swiveled to him. He looked grim but nodded at Tarek. He had done what he was supposed to do. Tarek nodded back.

Wren slipped in behind him, looking even worse than Joseph. She too nodded at Tarek and then went to stand beside Karn. She was letting him know that she trusted him. Now was the time for solidarity, not division.

A loud boom shook the room. Everyone jumped and looked at Ibris, wanting him to answer the question that would make all the difference in their plans.

Was that the storm or Sawdi dropping out of time? It mattered. They needed the storm to be first.

Fifty-Five

Stryker stumbled in the darkness and swore to himself. The darkness was making this harder. Of course, it was also hiding him in case someone figured out that he had escaped.

The first boom almost knocked him off his feet. Storm or Sawdi, both were dangerous. The ziffering captain of the Soleis better wait for him. He had to get off the Islands before Sawdi found him.

Feeling along the wall, he followed the dot on the map until it showed him that the pendant piece was on the other side of the wall.

Within seconds he found the door, and after a moment of confusion, discovered the pendant wrapped in cloth under the floorboards. He had no time to appreciate it or even gloat over the fact that he had tricked Karn. He had to hurry. They would be coming for him to help them stop Sawdi any minute, and would discover his absence. It was time to go.

It took only a few minutes until Stryker found the door of the building and flung himself outside. Flashing lighting, whipping winds, and another blast of thunder told him that he had lucked out. The storm was here first, but the rain had not yet arrived even though the skies were dark enough. It was the gods favoring him again and letting him get to the ship.

Falcon appeared above him, lit by the flash of lightning, and started flying in the direction of the harbor. Stryker followed as quickly as he could, tripping over tree roots and getting scratched by every bramble bush on the way.

If Stryker didn't know that Falcon was under his command, he might have worried that Falcon was taking him the hardest way. But he knew that wasn't the case. They were going the fastest way. He could heal up once he got to the boat.

A few minutes later, he found the steps cut into the cliff and saw a rowboat bobbing on the waves below. He shouted, and someone waved. Getting down the steps wasn't easy in the dark, but the constant lightning flashes saved him from being in total darkness.

The wind was blowing so hard that there were moments when he felt as if it would sweep him off the steps. Amazingly the rain still hadn't come. Once again, Stryker thanked the gods, whoever they were, for taking care of him.

Two men stepped out of the rowboat and helped him navigate the waves. He made it harder for them because he didn't offer both hands. One hand was clutching the pendant. He would rather drown than let it go.

Eventually, they made it to the ship, and Stryker lay on the deck shivering in the cold. Above him, the sky split open, and he watched as five dragons and the white mass that he knew were Warrior Monks headed to the Temple.

The ship was already out of the harbor and on its way. He had to do the one thing he could do. He cloaked the boat. He couldn't do it for long, but it was long enough so that no one would see them leaving the Island.

Sawdi had arrived. But he was too late. He would destroy the Islands, believing that he had also killed Stryker.

Someday he might figure out what had happened, but the map had shown him where the next part of the pendant was, and that was where he would head. When he found it, he would have enough power to stop anyone, including Sawdi and his Warrior Monks.

Stryker took the blanket and hot drink offered him by one of the crew and walked to the bow of the ship and stared out across the ocean. He was safe.

****

"Is he gone?" Karn asked Tarek.

"Yes," Tarek answered. "Are you ready?" he asked the room.

The only answers he got were silent nods. Wren, Roar, and Ruth stood together, holding hands.

Tarek had met Wren outside the room and told her what he had done. At first, Wren wanted to slap him. Didn't he know he could trust her? When she realized that he had done it to keep her safe, she conceded that he had done the right thing.

As Wren stood with Ruth and Roar, Karn stood behind her with his hands on her shoulders. She allowed herself to lean slightly back into him. And he tightened his grip in response. Their plan had to work. He needed to prove to Wren that she could trust him.

Leon and his men headed towards the door, preparing to leave, while the Mages made a circle around Ibris.

Meg turned to her sister and said, "Be careful, please."

Suzanne kissed Meg on the cheek and said, "Always. See you soon." A few seconds later, they all watched as a dragon lit by a flash of lightning rose in the sky, heading for the Temple.

Meg started to cry. She knew that she might never see Suzanne again, but she also knew that for the first time since coming to the Islands, Suzanne felt free. What a sacrifice she had made by coming here, and now she was doing it again.

Tarek leaned down and whispered, "She'll be fine. She knows what she is doing."

A loud boom shook the room. Sawdi had arrived.

Fifty-Six

Sawdi barely let Bolong's feet touch the ground before leaping off and running towards the Temple. Just as he suspected, the remaining Kai-Via were praying in the Temple, foreheads to the floor bowing towards Aaron. Sawdi knew they were trying to hide their trembling, but it didn't matter. It pleased him to see their fear.

The six of them rose as they heard Sawdi's footsteps and waited, arms crossed, hands tucked inside their sleeves, heads bowed. If Dax had been there, it would have been him that would have greeted Sawdi. Now, none of them knew who should say anything, so instead, they stayed silent.

"Oh for zut's sake, speak," Sawdi yelled, kicking the nearest man. "Where are they? Where are Dax, Ibris, and Stryker?"

"Gone, master," the Kai-Via he had kicked whispered. "We can't find them."

Sawdi roared. It felt good. He knew they would have run from the Temple, he expected that they would go into hiding, but he didn't want to give the man a break. He wanted him to feel as if the world was coming to an end. Which it was—their world.

The Warrior Monks would find them. Nothing would escape

their slithering throughout the landscape. They had orders to bring the three missing men back to the Temple alive. What they did with the rest, he didn't care. At the last minute, he had told them to save the women for Aaron. He would bring them back to him as a gift.

He knew what Aaron was up to with the women of the Blessed Ones. It didn't matter. Let him have his fun. It kept Aaron distracted, along with his gold and jewels. The people could worship that fool for a little while longer. At least Aaron wasn't betraying him, like Dax, Ibris, and that fool Stryker.

Stryker, he would not keep around. At least not for long. Just long enough to have a little pleasure with him. But his ruling days were over. Just as these six Kai-Via's days were too if they didn't keep doing what he wanted them to do.

"Bring up the conversion pool," Sawdi said. "I'm in the mood for a little swimming."

One of the Kai-Via hustled off to do what he asked as the other five waited for their orders.

"What are you waiting for, help him. Get it done. And add all those drugs that Dax has been adding to the water. It will make it even more fun."

After the six had gone, Sawdi strode to the back of the Temple and waited for the pool to appear. For the first time in days, he was by himself. The Warrior Monks were seeking, and the dragons waited outside in the storm. For a moment, the thought that the dragons could use some shelter occurred to him, but he dismissed the idea. A little storm wouldn't hurt them.

On his finger, Sawdi's ring was pulsing. Demanding. The ring itself looked so ordinary and worthless.

None of the boys had paid any attention to it when they first saw it—only him. Aaron and Stryker were bedazzled by the bright gold and jewels that they had found buried in the forest outside the school. They never saw the ring. It wasn't flashy enough.

The three of them had found the little box by accident. They had been chasing some of the boys from the school through the woods when Aaron tripped over a stone. He had fallen hard enough that they had stopped the chase and come to his side.

It was Stryker who had noticed the opening under the stone, and the three boys had pushed and pulled at it until it rolled away, revealing the box. Aaron claimed it was all his. After all, he had been the one to find it.

"As if being a clumsy idiot qualifies as finding," Stryker had lashed back.

Sawdi had not participated in the dividing of spoils. He had noticed something fall out of the box and roll away, and it felt as if it called to him. Even then, he was aware that it was more than a piece of jewelry. Turning so that no one could see what he was doing, he picked up the ring and slid it onto his finger.

At first, nothing happened, and he wondered if he had been wrong. It was only when he turned to look at his friends that he realized what was different. They were the same. Boys, delighted with the gold and jewels as if they meant something. They were the same. He had changed. He saw things differently.

That's all he knew at the time. He had no idea what he was seeing as waves and threads of energy pulsed around him. But he liked it and decided to never tell anyone about it.

Instead, he practiced doing things with those threads and waves. Sometimes what he did almost killed him by mistake as he directed them towards himself instead of away.

But in time, he had learned to use them to do things like change the scenery to fit what he wanted to see and eventually to raise the dead and direct them to do his bidding. Or the ring's bidding. But that was not something that he wanted to admit. Sometimes the ring was not happy with him and let him know about it. So to please the ring, he gave it more. And what it wanted was life.

That was why he had helped design Aaron-Lem. The destroying of the people and their villages pleased the ring. When it got too peaceful, the ring had not liked it, which was why he had been happy to bring back the dead and come after Stryker. It made the ring happy, and that meant he was happy too.

Once, he had tried to take the ring off. And he couldn't. He and the ring were one now. There was nothing he could do about it but enjoy what the ring wanted because he wanted it too.

As he waited for the Warrior Monks to return, Sawdi sighed with pleasure. The only thing that ever worried him was the small sound he had heard the day he had found the ring. Had someone seen him with it?

Sawdi sighed again. It didn't matter. They were probably dead by now anyway.

Fifty-Seven

Meg closed her eyes even though she knew not looking would not protect anyone. But the noise was so loud it felt as if it was eating into her bones and shaking them out of her body. She knew everyone else was experiencing the same thing, but they held each other tighter as the sound grew louder, trying not to let terror take over.

Outside, the storm lashed against the building, but even the winds and the frozen rain had not stopped the Warrior Monks. Through the window, the lightning flashes revealed the first wave of white wraiths heading towards them.

That's when Meg shut her eyes—seeing them made it worse. She could tell that they were coming closer because the humming sound increased. And if they had feelings, it sounded as if they were angry.

Leon and his men stood guard, looking helpless because they knew they had no power against what was coming. Dax stood with them, feeling more powerless than he had ever felt. His knife would be useless against the enemy that was coming for them.

He and Leon exchanged looks. Dax knew that Leon had a right to hate him, but it wasn't hate that he saw in his eyes. He saw understanding. Understanding that they would stand or fall together. It was also a look of pain. They were warriors, used to fighting. However, now all they could do was protect the people inside the room as long as possible. But there were no weapons that anyone knew that could stop the white wraiths, so the look was also an understanding that they would fail.

The only thing they could do was hide. In plain sight. And that was what they were doing. Hiding. But not just themselves. They were hiding every person on both Hetale and Lopel.

Every person in the room who had any magical ability was sending it to the Mages, Ibris, and Tarek as they produced an invisibility shield over every living thing on the Islands.

It was a mammoth task, made even harder because the people on the Islands did not know that they were being shielded. They would hear and see the white cloud sweep across the land and believe that it was the end of the world for them.

Meg's heart felt as if it would burst out of her chest, worrying about the people who didn't know what was happening. Would they die of terror? Would they clutch each other and pray to Aaron to save them, still believing that Aaron was a real God? She could not help the Mages with what they were doing. She had no power to help hold the shield over the Islands.

Tarek and Ibris stood with the Mages doing the impossible. Dax was with Leon and his men. Karn, Wren, Roar, and Ruth faced each other in a circle, heads bowed, foreheads touching, adding to the power of the Mages. Silke sat on Tarek's shoulder, blinking on and off faster than Meg had ever seen her do before.

Everyone was so busy doing what they had to do, that no one had noticed that Meg now stood alone, eyes closed, asking to be of service in some way, but shaking so hard she was barely standing.

It was Karn who noticed what was happening and threw himself at Meg. He dragged her to the center of the circle of Mages. Within seconds Meg stood in a column of fire. And then with one mighty whoosh, a column of light burst from her and traveled straight up through the roof.

Inside the room, the humming stopped. Even the storm had stilled.

****

Outside the Temple, Suzanne coasted above the storm, waiting for the Warrior Monks to move on through the Islands. If they saw her, she would die. She had no defenses against the wraiths. She was here to contact the dragons, but she didn't know if the dragons waiting below would see her as a threat or a friend. There was only one way to find out.

Silently, Suzanne glided to the ground a few hundred feet from where the five dragons huddled together. When one of them looked up, his eyes flaring, she had a moment of terror. She shifted to a woman and then back again, hoping he would understand.

****

Bolong blinked. Was it possible? Was there another dragon in Thamon? A woman shapeshifter? He lowered his head and closed his eyes, trying to signal that he was not dangerous. The dragon shifted back to a woman and walked over to the five of them. The other four had noticed her too but kept still, following Bolong's lead.

"Hello," Suzanne said, to who she believed to be the head of the crown. "Can you talk to me?"

When the dragon tilted his head but didn't speak, she tried again, but this time she pushed the thought into his head. For Bolong, it was as if a light flicked on, and hope flared in his heart. Perhaps this was the help he had prayed for.

"Sawdi will be coming out soon, and he will be angry. But if you like, my friends and I can help you."

"How?" Bolong asked.

"I will be following you and will be a messenger between you and the Mages and Wizards who are protecting the Islands now. They will fight to overthrow the three men who control Thamon. Will you join us?"

For Bolong and the other four dragons, it was the moment they had been praying for. For the first time since Sawdi had locked them into dragon form, they had help.

"Yes," was the resounding answer from all five of them.

Fifty-Eight

The wraiths returned to the Temple in a thick mass, buzzing louder than Sawdi had ever heard them. They slid through the walls of the Temple until they filled the space. The six Kai-Via, seeing them arrive, had hidden behind the secret front wall of the Temple, hoping somehow that would save them.

The wraiths packed the Temple, floating over the surface of the pool, empty black eyes all looking towards Sawdi, who stood alone near the Temple's main doors.

A Monk separated himself from the mass and hovered directly in front of Sawdi. For a moment, there was complete silence, and then Sawdi lifted his face and roared. The Warrior Monks hummed louder, sending waves of sound across the Islands, and out to sea.

The conversion pool waters splashed onto the floors, the walls of the Temple shook and began to crack. Sawdi roared louder, and one Temple wall fell and then another. Outside, the dragons rose in the air to stay safe, and Suzanne ran into the surrounding woods.

She had seen the column of light and smiled. Finally, it had happened. She had heard myths and stories about someone in their family who would bring the power of light. She didn't know it would be Meg, but as Meg had lost her ability to shapeshift in the dark, and gained an understanding and loving heart in return, Suzanne had wondered if Meg was the one. Now she knew.

Suzanne wanted to fly back to the building and be there for her sister, but it wasn't possible. Her task was already set. She would see Meg again, and rejoice together after they freed Thamon.

Many miles out to sea, the crew of the Soleis and Stryker heard the roar and scrambled to the deck to see what caused it.

Stryker didn't need to look. He knew it was Sawdi, and he trembled in fear. He had to find the last part of the pendant before Sawdi found him.

He couldn't believe that Karn had betrayed him. Again. He hadn't been on the ship waiting for him, ready to stand by his side as he fought Sawdi. But what did he expect? Betrayal was a game they were all playing. The question was who would win.

The captain of the Soleis touched Stryker's shoulder and pointed to Lopel. Rising from the Island was a column of light. It spread out over the Island as they all watched, flashed, and then it was gone.

What the ziffer was that, Stryker thought? *Not Sawdi. Not the Warrior Monks. One of the Mages? No,* Stryker thought, *there has never been someone who could do that on Thamon.* Now he had something else to fear, something he didn't know about and didn't understand.

Stryker turned to the captain and yelled, "We have to move, and fast."

The captain didn't need to be told twice. Neither did the men. They had seen the white mass descend, heard the roar, and now saw the column of light. Danger was heading their way, but it didn't know where they were.

They had a secret they had kept from their passenger. And that secret would keep them safe for now. They would take Stryker to the mainland. After that, he was not their problem.

Falcon watched the scrambling of the men, heard the noise, saw the light, and if a falcon could smile, he did.

The captain looked up and saluted. Falcon tipped his head to the side in acknowledgment. He had learned many things from Stryker. One of them was the art of betrayal.

****

It's impossible, Sawdi thought after screaming his rage. He had found the six Kai-Via, apparently the only remaining people on the Islands, and thrown them into the pool. The wraiths held them down, and the men slowly sank to the bottom. It was what he had intended to do anyway, but he had hoped to enjoy the process more.

Now he was in a rush. He had to find out where the people had gone. Actually, he didn't care about the people, although they might become a problem. He only cared about Stryker. How had he escaped? Had he helped the people flee, too?

For now, he chose not worry about the people of the Islands because he had no idea where they had gone. He would have to return to the Palace and regroup.

If he could discover where the last part of the pendant was, he would find Stryker there. No need to chase him around Thamon. He would simply lie in waiting for him.

The rage at what had happened built up again, and he released another roar as he jumped onto Bolong, and jabbing him in the ribs with his knife, pushed him into the air. The Warrior Monks surrounded them, and with a blast of fire, the dragons pushed off.

Suzanne watched them go and then shifted to follow as a dragon. Bolong had told her where they were going, and since she didn't know how to travel outside of time, she would go to the dragon's cave, where the dragons would be waiting for her, and they would plan what to do next.

****

"Are they gone?" Meg croaked. She had woken to find herself lying on a cot in the main room, covered in blankets. Tarek was sitting on a chair, holding her hand. Silke was fluttering around so much her feathered hair was sticking almost entirely up in the air. Seeing that Meg was awake, she settled down on to the blankets, blinking steadily.

Leon and his men had formed a circle around the cot, looking both proud and worried at the same time. Ruth sat on the other side of the bed, holding a cup of hot water, and as Meg tried to speak, she helped her sip the water.

"Yes, they are gone."

"And the people?"

"Everyone is safe, Meg," Tarek answered. "Suzanne contacted the dragons and will keep an eye on Sawdi and the wraiths as planned. At the moment, they are heading back to Aaron's Palace. Probably to regroup and figure out where Stryker went."

Meg sat up on the cot, holding the cup of water. "So the plan worked? Stryker found the pendant that Wren hid and then ran away. The captain of the Soleis waited for him?"

Wren nodded. "He did. Falcon and Karn are old friends, and we know where Stryker is going even though Sawdi does not."

Karn pulled a chair up beside Wren and said, "You did it, Meg. Whatever you did scared the Warrior Monks, and they returned to the Temple and refused to continue on the Islands.

"Sawdi was furious, but what could he do? The Monks told him that there were no people on the Islands, that they had all escaped, and that Stryker was on the run. There was nothing here for him, so he left."

Meg swung her legs around until they hung off the cot, hands braced against the side, her dark hair hanging over her face as she looked at the floor.

Lifting her face to the group, Meg said, "Okay. I'm ready. Someone tell me what happened."

Fifty-Nine

Tarek found Meg standing outside the building, her cloak pulled tightly around herself, her hair flying in the wind, and tears running down her face. Meg swiped the tears away when she saw Tarek, but couldn't hide the sadness in her face.

When Tarek pulled her in close, wrapping his cloak around her, she started crying again. He waited until she stopped before holding her at arm's length and bending down, so he was looking directly into her eyes.

"Are you ready, Meg?"

"Ready. But afraid. And sad. And worried. And confused. And happy," Meg answered. "How can I be all those things at one time?"

Putting his hands on both sides of her face as he looked into her eyes, Tarek answered, "What happened is a lot to take in, Meg, so it's not surprising that you feel all those things. You used to escape those feelings by telling yourself that you didn't care, and being what Suzanne called you, a wild child.

"Now, you are so much more than that. Without your help, we couldn't have saved the Islands."

"But, I don't know how I did that, or how to do it again, or what it was. I am grateful that it happened, and that everyone is safe, but what was that? Will it happen again? What if it happens when it is not supposed to, and I make something bad happen?"

Before Tarek had a chance to answer, Leon appeared with Silke. "It's time to go," Leon said.

As they turned to follow him, Tarek reached for Meg's hand and said, "Have faith, Meg. We will find the answers to your questions, and I am positive that you will only ever be able to use it for good."

Silke nodded in agreement, and Meg's eyes filled up again. Would she ever stop crying?

Inside the room, there was more crying along with outbursts of laughter. There was joy that the danger was over, at least for now, and sorrow that they would be saying goodbye to people who had become comrades and friends. The women were hugging each other, and the men were slapping each other on their backs, as they said goodbye to each other.

The group had divided itself into those who were staying and those who were going. At first, everyone wanted to go after Stryker, Aaron, and Sawdi.

But it was Wren, once more taking the lead, who said no. The people of the Islands would need some of them, and it was Wren who chose who would leave and who would stay.

First, the Mages would stay. They were needed to protect the Islands. Ibris and Dax had to stay, too. They would need to help the people of the Islands adjust to the withdrawal of Aaron-Lem.

Dax knew that they would not only be withdrawing from the teachings, but also from the drugs that they had taken without their knowledge.

Nobody expected it to be a smooth, or easy, transition. But Ibris would use his gift of words to help the people return to their faiths and community that they had abandoned for Aaron-Lem. Dax would use his ability to make things happen to keep order.

Nobody believed that Dax would find it easy to be a warrior turned peacemaker, but Ibris had said that he had faith in his cousin, and Tarek agreed.

Leon, Tarek, Ibris, and Dax had met separately and talked about family. For Tarek, it had been especially emotional. For years, he thought that Leon was the only member of his family left, and finding Ibris and Dax had filled his heart with hope that perhaps he would discover more of his family. Of all their families.

One worry that they all had was, were the ones who had gone into hiding were still safe. Part of their next mission was to ensure that they were.

Samis had come to the building to say goodbye, and he promised to help Dax. It burned his throat to say so, but he meant it. He would trust that Dax had transformed, and act that way, but he would still keep an eye on what he did.

Ruth and Roar stood off to the side, waiting. They were heartbroken. They were staying, and Wren was going. What would they do without her? They knew why she was going, and they knew why she had said they had to stay.

Wren was trying to keep them safe, and the Islands were the safest place that they could be. Oiseon joined Ruth and Roar as they watched the goodbyes and leaned in to say, "Wren will be fine, and we'll be your family until she returns. And long past that if you'll have us."

As Etar rose in the east, the last of the goodbyes were said. Those that were leaving headed to the harbor on Lopel, where the Eos was waiting for them. The same ship that had brought Tarek to the Islands, and now would be taking him away. But this time, Tarek was bringing help.

Lira, the captain of the Eos, greeted Tarek with a hug and welcomed Leon and his men. Of course, he knew them all. He had brought them to the Islands too, along with Stryker.

Captain Lira and his men had taken the Mages to safety and then returned to wait until they were needed again. Sometimes sailing away out of the path of the storms, but always returning close enough for Silke to find them.

"Thanks for waiting for us," Tarek said.

"Well," Captain Lira said, "You know we only waited for Leon. We've missed his cooking!"

A mile out to sea, two ravens landed on one of Eos's masts. They stayed long enough to see everyone settle in and to make sure that their beloved friend, Wren, was safe.

As they lifted off, Wren called after them, "Goodbye, dear friends. We'll be back!" Beside her, Karn reached for her hand, and she accepted it.

Tarek and Meg stood together watching as Etar and Trin crossed each other on the horizon. For a moment there was a flash of blue light. A good omen. Wren was right, they would be back, and Thamon's people would be free.

****

Udore felt Aaron's presence long before he arrived outside his cell door. He knew that sooner or later, Aaron would come to ask him for his help. And that time had come.

His years of living in the dark cell buried beneath Aaron's Palace were coming to an end. Yes, he would accept Aaron's offer of helping him. Yes, it would be to save his son, Tarek. But not in the way that Aaron believed.

Udore had never lost faith that someday he would be given a

chance to defeat Aaron-Lem, and now that time was near.

Alone in his cell, he had felt the burst of light emanating from somewhere on the planet, and hope had flared in his heart. The prophecy was being fulfilled.

As Aaron unlocked his cell door, Udore stood and waited. Looking grim, but smiling within.

He knew something Aaron didn't know. His son was alive, he was coming, and he was bringing help.

After Betrayed, What's Next?

Join me in the next book in this series, *Discovered*.

There are so many questions that need to be answered.

What's up with Meg? What does Karn know? Is it something that can stop Sawdi? Whose side is Falcon on? Will Stryker find the pendant? And if he does, what happens?

What about the love stories going on? Tarek and Meg. Karn and Wren. Is there another love story in the works? Answer. Yes, there is! Who do you think it's between?

Thank you for joining me as I reveal the answers to these questions and many more. I promise, if you loved this story, you will love the next one too!

PS.

Be the first to know when there are new books. Join my mailing list at becalewis.com/fantasy, and get the free short story that answers so many questions about how the *Karass, Erda,* and *Thamon* series are related. Yes, Suzanne is in all of them. How is that possible?

Author's Note

Writing a book is always a discovery for me. Yes, I know what the theme of the book is, and yes, I know the basics of it before I start writing. But unlike writers who can outline a book before they write it, if I wait for a full outline, I will never get started.

Instead, I have to sit down each day and trust that there is a story waiting for me to tell it. Some people call those of us who write this way, pantsers, implying that we are writing without knowing what's happening.

Joanna Penn calls it being a discovery writer. This is a much better term. As a discovery writer, I become a discoverer of a story that is waiting to be told. If I can stay out of my own way, the story unfolds for me just as it does as a reader.

If I can stay in that open mind, I see what is happening, and I write it down. Later I can go back and correct my mistakes, but that's a different state of mind that does that. I enjoy editing too. I love cleaning things up and making them orderly — even words.

When I was a choreographer, I worked the same way. I worked out how many beats I needed for the musical phrases of movement, the same way I work out how many chapters deal with the phases of the story. Then I wait for the movement to unfold in my head.

Same, same, as one of my granddaughters would say as she compared two similar things.

Thank you for reading my books. Otherwise, it would just be me and the words, and although words are lovely, it's the sharing of them that makes it all worthwhile.

******

Connect with me online:
Twitter: http://twitter.com/becalewis
Facebook: https://www.facebook.com/becalewiscreative
Facebook: https://www.facebook.com/becalewisfans
Pinterest: https://www.pinterest.com/theshift/
Instagram: http://instagram.com/becalewis
LinkedIn: https://linkedin.com/in/becalewis

ACKNOWLEDGMENTS

I could never write a book without the help of my friends and my book community. Thank you Jet Tucker, Jamie Lewis, Diana Cormier, Barbara Budan and Heidi Christianson for taking the time to do the final reader proof. You can't imagine how much I appreciate it.

A huge thank you to Laura Moliter for her fantastic book editing.

Thank you to the fabulous Molly Phipps at wegotyoucoveredbookdesign.com for the beautiful book covers for the *Erda* series.

Thank you to every other member of my Book Community who help me make so many decisions that help the book be the best book possible.

Thank you to all the people who tell me that they love to read these stories. Those random comments from friends and strangers are more valuable than gold.

And as always, thank you to my beloved husband, Del, for being my daily sounding board, for putting up with all my questions, my constant need to want to make things better, and for being the love of my life, in more than just this one lifetime.

OTHER BECA BOOKS

The Karass Chronicles - Magical Realism
Karass, Pragma, Jatismar, Exousia, Stemma, Paragnosis

The Return To Erda Series - Fantasy
Shatterskin, Deadsweep, Abbadon

The Chronicles of Thamon - Fantasy
Banished, Betrayed, Discovered

The Shift Series - Spiritual Self-Help
Living in Grace: The Shift to Spiritual Perception
The Daily Shift: Daily Lessons From Love To Money
The 4 Essential Questions: Choosing Spiritually Healthy
Habits
The 28 Day Shift To Wealth: A Daily Prosperity Plan
The Intent Course: Say Yes To What Moves You
Imagination Mastery: A Workbook For Shifting Your Reality

Perception Parables: - Fiction - very short stories
Love's Silent Sweet Secret: A Fable About Love
Golden Chains And Silver Cords: A Fable About Letting Go

Advice: - Nonfiction
A Woman's ABC's of Life: Lessons in Love, Life and Career
from Those Who Learned The Hard Way

ABOUT BECA LEWIS

Beca writes books that she hopes will change people's perceptions of themselves and the world, and open possibilities to things and ideas that are waiting to be seen and experienced.

At sixteen, Beca founded her own dance studio. Later, she received a Master's Degree in Dance in Choreography from UCLA and founded the Harbinger Dance Theatre, a multimedia dance company, while continuing to run her dance school.

After graduating—to better support her three children— Beca switched to the sales field, where she worked as an employee and independent contractor to many industries, excelling in each while perfecting and teaching her Shift® system, and writing books.

She joined the financial industry in 1983 and became an Associate Vice President of Investments at a major stock brokerage firm, and was a licensed Certified Financial Planner for more than twenty years.

This diversity, along with a variety of life challenges, helped fuel the desire to share what she's learned by writing and talking with the hope that it will make a difference in other people's lives.

Beca grew up in State College, PA, with the dream of becoming a dancer and then a writer. She carried that dream forward as she fulfilled a childhood wish by moving to Southern

California in 1969. Beca told her family she would never move back to the cold.

After living there for thirty years, she met her husband Delbert Lee Piper, Sr., at a retreat in Virginia, and everything changed. They decided to find a place they could call their own which sent them off traveling around the United States. For a year or so they lived and worked in a few different places before returning to live in the cold once again near Del's family in a small town in Northeast Ohio, not too far from State College.

When not working and teaching together, they love to visit and play with their combined family of eight children and five grandchildren, read, study, do yoga or taiji, feed birds, work in their garden, and design things. Actually, designing things is what Beca loves to do. Del enjoys the end result.